Praise for *Dead-End M*

A *New York Times* Notable Book
An NPR Best Book of the Year
A *Bustle* Most Anticipated Book of the Month
A *Millions* Most Anticipated Book of the Year
A *Literary Hub* Most Anticipated Book of the Year

"*Dead-End Memories* is a collection of stories, each of which, while specific and distinct, has at its center a woman both losing and finding something of herself. In Asa Yoneda's elegant translation of this collection—whose title story Yoshimoto herself considers her best—the soothing rhythm of the everyday and the mundane is broken by equally quiet moments of profundity." —Ilana Masad, an NPR Best Book of the Year

"This collection offers plenty of Yoshimoto's signature themes: lonely women, betrayal, relationship upsets—and grace, too." —*The New York Times*

"Nineteen years have passed between *Dead-End Memories*' original publication in Japan in 2003 and its arrival in the United States in 2022. The translation of this volume from Japanese into English was well worth the wait. Yoshimoto offers five stories that read like tiny miracles, facilitated by Asa Yoneda's thoughtful translation. Even when Yoshimoto's characters face tragedy or due reason for hopelessness, they quietly find a path toward hope." —*Harper's Bazaar*

"Once upon a time, Yoshimoto (born 1964) debuted as one of Japan's youngest literary phenoms. In the decades since, she continues to produce brilliantly relevant fiction, notable for an open, accessible simplicity that belies revelatory observations about life, love, happiness, and more . . . Her latest collection contains five short stories translated again by Yoneda, who English-enabled Yoshimoto's novel *Moshi Moshi* (2016). Each tale features women examining significant relationships, and each involves food-related settings—restaurants, cafeterias, a bar—seeming to suggest emotional needs transformed into something achingly physical . . . Bittersweet yet radiant, poignant yet promising, Yoshimoto once again showcases her dazzling appeal." —*Booklist* (starred review)

"Yoshimoto's resonant collection centers on women struggling through challenging events. Though the characters in each of the five stories have been struck by bad luck and duplicity, they are intrinsically good-natured and are also greatly influenced by the generational traditions of their forebears . . . Yoshimoto embellishes these gorgeously written gems with sensual descriptions of food and sex, and makes them memorable by showing how the women set themselves free from misfortune via friendship and resilience. This is a gem."

—*Publishers Weekly* (starred review)

"These stories made me believe again that it was possible to write honestly, rigorously, morally, about the material reality of characters; to write toward human warmth as a reaffirmation of the bonds that tie us together. This is a supremely hopeful book, one that feels important because it shows that happiness, while not always easy, is still a subject worthy of art."

—Brandon Taylor, *The New York Times Book Review*

"Deftly translated by Bristol-based translator Asa Yoneda, *Dead-End Memories* contains five stories exploring the lives of five women struggling through challenging events. The dreamy, sometimes surreal stories explore emotionally heavy-hitting themes like life, love, death, happiness, identity, loneliness and grief, delivered with the author's characteristic light touch. In other words, it's classic Yoshimoto— great news for existing fans . . . One of the great pleasures of reading Yoshimoto is her gift for creating exceptional imagery out of simple language . . . Like your average lo-fi playlist, this is a late-night read to heighten a melancholy, nostalgic or contemplative state of mind, one you dive into to be transported to a kinder, gentler world for an hour or two."

—Florentyna Leow, *Japan Times*

"Available for the first time in English, this collection of five stories about extraordinarily ordinary women facing hardships is a wonderful introduction to her masterful work."   —Karla J. Strand, *Ms.*

"Yoshimoto's writing style is economical. Most of her protagonists are, at heart, well-meaning people. And her stories assert, unabashedly, that good stories don't have to have unhappy endings."

—Alison Fincher, *Asian Review of Books*

"Yoshimoto gracefully explores the beauties and sorrows of everyday life, offering an overall feeling of hope and gentleness that is refreshing in our current times."

—*Electric Literature*, a Best Book of the Year

"*Dead-End Memories* follows several women, each one coming back to her life after a traumatic event. Although you will find heartbreak, ghosts, and betrayal humming in the background of these tales, you will also encounter a great deal of heart and optimism. Don't we all need that right now? It's the kind of collection that leaves you a little lighter."

—Katie Yee, a *Literary Hub* Most Anticipated Book of the Year

"A new short story collection from one of Japan's most beloved authors features five women seeking peace in the face of uncertainty . . . One of the things that separates Yoshimoto from many contemporary writers is her refusal to linger on her characters' dark nights of the soul: All her protagonists are ultimately changed irrevocably by kindnesses—from others, from the natural world, from themselves—that lead them on paths toward the light. This, coupled with

Yoshimoto's gentle prose (translated here by Yoneda), makes the collection perfect for readers looking for stories that will leave a sweet taste in their mouths without sacrificing depth or intelligence."

—*Kirkus Reviews*

"Banana Yoshimoto is one of our greatest writers; in *Dead-End Memories*, she is absolutely at her best. Written with tenderness, complexity, generosity, and warmth, Yoshimoto's characters are entirely singular, and also a finely wrought reflection of ourselves. This book is masterful—a portrait of the absurdity, brilliance, horror, and love encompassing daily life—and, in her delivery, Yoshimoto is a master." —Bryan Washington, author of *Memorial*

"Reading Banana Yoshimoto is like taking a bracing, cleansing bath. These gentle yet formidable stories in *Dead-End Memories* rinse away the unimportant minutiae of life, leaving behind only the essential."

—Ling Ma, author of *Severance*

"Yoshimoto's stories are led by women who do not perfectly fit the 'hero' archetype. None are etched with glory or divine purpose. Instead, they breathe, make mistakes, and experience profound loneliness, failure, tragedy, and loss within a society that carries on and spares them with no second thought. Sad and almost darkly comedic, these women struggle to form deeper connections in an industrialized global society that strives to erase individuality. The meaning that this compelling collection seems to embody is the appreciation and innate need for human warmth. The bonds that tie people together make life ultimately meaningful. After all, it is only a matter of time before the leaves change color and the current picks up to sweep us along with it."

—Ella Kelleher, *Asia Media International*

Dead-End Memories

ALSO BY BANANA YOSHIMOTO

Kitchen

N.P.

Lizard

Amrita

Asleep

Goodbye Tsugumi

Argentine Hag

Hardboiled & Hard Luck

The Lake

Moshi Moshi

Dead-End Memories

Stories

Banana Yoshimoto

TRANSLATED FROM THE JAPANESE
BY ASA YONEDA

Counterpoint
Berkeley, California

First Counterpoint edition: 2022
First paperback edition: 2023
English translation copyright © 2022 by Asa Yoneda
Deddoendo no omoide by Banana Yoshimoto
Copyright © 2003 by Banana Yoshimoto

Originally published in Japan by Bungeishunju Ltd.
English translation rights arranged with Banana Yoshimoto through ZIPANGO, S.L. and Michael Kevin Staley.

The Library of Congress has cataloged the hardcover edition as follows:
Names: Yoshimoto, Banana, 1964– author. | Yoneda, Asa, translator.
Title: Dead-end memories : stories / Banana Yoshimoto ; translated from the Japanese by Asa Yoneda.
Other titles: Deddoendo no omoide. English
Description: First Counterpoint edition. | Berkeley, California : Counterpoint, 2022.
Identifiers: LCCN 2022008903 | ISBN 9781640093690 (hardcover) | ISBN 9781640093706 (ebook)
Subjects: LCGFT: Short stories.
Classification: LCC PL865.O7138 D4313 2022 | DDC 895.63/5—dc23/
eng/20220224
LC record available at https://lccn.loc.gov/2022008903

Paperback ISBN: 978-1-64009-610-3

Cover design by Dana Li
Cover art: gingko leaves © istockphoto.com / Mantonature;
istockphoto.com / Stefan Sutka
Book design by Wah-Ming Chang

COUNTERPOINT
2560 Ninth Street, Suite 318
Berkeley, CA 94710
www.counterpointpress.com

Printed in the United States of America

3 5 7 9 10 8 6 4 2

For Fujiko F. Fujio

Contents

Dead-End Memories

House of Ghosts

"I'll have hot pot, if you're offering. But eating alone's no fun, so why don't you join me?"

What I'd said was "Can I treat you to a meal as a thank-you for all those times you had my back at work?"

And that was what Iwakura said in response.

I wasn't quite sure how to take an invitation like that from a boy who had his own apartment.

This is Iwakura we're talking about, I thought. *He probably doesn't mean anything by it.* He'd already mentioned his building was nearby.

And in any case he said it so casually, and with such an artless expression, that my heart didn't give a single flutter.

Iwakura had an intriguing mixture of bright and dark about him, like a cloudy midwinter sky,

3

which had somehow made me hold back from starting to like him. I couldn't see him giving me that heady feeling, the rush that makes you want to burst into a run—the things I was looking for in young love.

"I'll come over and cook," I said, and we picked a date, matter-of-factly.

We were by the bench under the tall zelkova on our college campus.

I didn't have a lot of friends, and the few that I did have were too busy with their part-time jobs to come to class much. It was the kind of thing that happened at low-tier private colleges like ours. So Iwakura and I had naturally become close simply from being two loners on campus.

We'd met when I was covering some shifts for a friend at a local place that served drinks and food where he worked behind the bar.

After that, we'd stop to chat or eat lunch together whenever we saw each other on campus.

His parents ran a famous bakery in our town that sold high-end cake rolls. He'd told me how, as the only child, he was doing everything in his power to save up enough money to avoid having to take over the family business after graduation. I believed him. There was a desperation about him that spoke of the lifetime of baking cake rolls that awaited him by default unless he forged his own path. He went about his part-time job like someone who had his work cut out for him.

"Cake rolls! What's not to like? They're great," I said, having never turned down a cake roll in my life.

"I don't mind the cake rolls, but my mom's practically perfect. Friendly, thoughtful, hardworking . . ." Iwakura said.

It was true that his mom was well known in the community for being welcoming and attentive. People ended up buying cake rolls at their bakery just because of how she made them feel.

"I . . . I think I'm quite a nice person," he said.

"I agree."

His gentle spirit and his good upbringing were obvious to me even just from our walks together. If we were in the park and the trees swayed in the wind and made the light dance, he would half-close his eyes and look blissful. If a child tripped and fell, he'd frown, and when the parent picked the child up afterward he'd look sympathetic and relieved. There was a candor about him I noticed in people whose parents had given them something unconditional and absolute growing up.

"If I stay home, with my family, for the rest of my life, I'll just get more and more *nice*."

"And that would be a problem because ..."

"It's fine, except the way I see it, it's not real. Anyone can be kind when they've got enough money and free time, and no problems, don't you think? What I'm saying is, if I stay at home, that's all my niceness will ever be. And either something dark and unpleasant starts building up inside me, or I'm stuck with that superficial niceness until I die. I'm lucky to be easygoing by nature, and I want to make sure that's what I feed. Not the dark stuff."

"That's why you're so desperate to save up and leave?"

"Maybe it's something like that. I'm just trying to look one step ahead. Otherwise I'll end up doing cake rolls without ever having known anything different. And then I'd really be stuck," Iwakura said.

The college we went to was expensive.

In my case, I ended up there because my parents

were both busy at the restaurant around the time I was born, and enrolled me in the kindergarten of the school attached to the college, where I'd come up through the system ever since.

My family ran a fairly well-known *yoshoku* restaurant in the next town over, which had been started by my grandparents. It was the kind of place listed in all the tourist guidebooks, where a family would stop by for a meal out, or a single office worker would go for a nice dinner after work when they didn't want to stretch for a French restaurant.

I wanted to run the place someday, so in truth I was more interested in learning to do that than in getting my degree. The restaurant's menu was unchanged from my grandparents' time, and I'd been trained from a young age to make things like *omurice*, pilaf, and demi-glace. All I really needed to do before I could take on the restaurant was to get my chef's license.

My elder brother had no interest in food, and had moved out on his own while he was still in high school. Now he had a busy and successful job at an advertising agency.

Iwakura's determination to do something— anything—other than go into the family business reminded me of my brother. Perhaps that was another reason I felt so close to him.

Back when we both still lived at home, my brother would often stay up late to vent his frustrations to me.

My brother loved people, and had an enormous sense of curiosity. He was always looking for excitement and loved surprises above everything. He was totally unsuited to a life of routine in which you needed to do the same thing, at the same time, in the same way, week in, week out. Only doting parents could have imagined he'd be the right person to run a restaurant.

"Leave it to me," I always told him. "It'll never work out for you."

On those nights, my brother would frown and try to talk himself into it, saying things like *But I'm better than you at working with my hands*, and *I like the idea of not being stuck behind a desk*, and *You know how happy it would make Mom and Dad . . .*

He was also the kind of person who liked to hold on to things he had, especially if other people wanted them.

After he moved out, all we'd see of him was when he'd drop by and stay for dinner before leaving again. He seemed to be enjoying his freedom and not planning on settling down anytime soon, and the chances of him coming back to run the restaurant when the time came seemed slim.

This evidently gave my parents something to chew on, and when I said I wanted to do it, they seemed to think I might be saying it out of a sense of obligation. To avoid making the same mistake they had made with my brother, they decided that I should be encouraged to spread my wings and see a little of the world first. It seemed to me they'd been seriously shaken by finding out that my brother, who they'd always assumed would succeed them, had disliked the idea quite so much all along.

So they sent me to college to give me time to think it over, and a chance to change my mind if I wanted to.

In any event, my feelings about it stayed exactly the same, so staying in school was turning out to be more of an opportunity to gain some life experience.

For me, being at the restaurant while my mom and dad grew older and eventually took on the roles of my old grandma, who had passed a while ago, and my grandpa, who still hung around like a mascot and visited with some of our oldest regulars when they came in, seemed like the surest and most important thing in my life. I didn't understand why my brother had been so against the idea that he had to move away from home to escape it.

Ever since I was young, I'd always stuck with things—maybe even taken them a little too far. I'd kept up my abacus until recently, and could still beat anyone at mental arithmetic. I'd been going to calligraphy lessons since I was a kid, and doing pottery as a hobby for more than a decade. I was even about to take a trip with three childhood friends to the same hot spring in Iwate we'd been to every year for the last eight years.

This was why I didn't know why Iwakura was so determined to turn his back on his family's bakery, whose position seemed as advantageous as their cake rolls were delicious. If he had his heart set on a different path, then maybe—but he had no plan. I couldn't understand what he was trying to do.

Because he wasn't the type to be forthcoming with the details of a situation, or his thoughts and feelings, it just sounded to me like he was giving up a sure thing in favor of pie in the sky.

That said, being from families that had been

serving customers for generations, we had a lot in common, and understood each other well.

Even if they didn't weigh too heavily on us, we couldn't help but be aware of the responsibilities we'd been born into.

On the day we'd chosen, I bought the ingredients for the hot pot and went to Iwakura's apartment for the very first time.

He'd told me that the building, which was already slated for demolition, stood on land owned by his uncle, who had agreed to let him live there in the meantime for a rent of five thousand yen a month. But somehow this hadn't prepared me for what I found.

The old wooden building was dilapidated, with broken windows, a crumbling outside staircase, and holes in the floors where the boards had rotted through.

I stopped in amazement. *Take a look at this*, I thought. *He lives here all on his own? I could never.*

Now that I'd seen the state the place was in, I understood why he was the only one living there.

I felt like I'd discovered the source of his peculiarly translucent darkness, the air of loneliness and heaviness that hung around him wherever he went.

I tightened my scarf, looked up at the clouded sky through the chilly winter air, and gulped. Something made me think I wouldn't be coming out of there the same as I went in.

I went up to the corner apartment on the second floor, and Iwakura opened the old sliding door and told me to come in.

"This is some place!"

"Isn't it? This room used to be the landlords' apartment, so it's bigger than the others."

He smiled.

It was true. Belying the impression I'd gotten from the small sliding door, the apartment easily contained two bedrooms, a kitchen, a living room, and a respectable-sized tatami room in the back. The ceilings were high, and the rear windows looked out onto a park where the evening chimes were just that moment ringing out from loudspeakers.

If you forgot that the other units were pitch dark and abandoned, it was a surprisingly bright and pleasant home.

"So, do you have a pot for this hot pot?" I asked.

"I do. And a picnic stove."

"It's going to be a simple dish of chicken meatballs, Chinese cabbage, and glass noodles. Are you happy with udon to finish?"

"This is a treat." Iwakura smiled.

"You know I'm much more used to cooking Western-style food. I can do that blindfolded."

"Of course, I can imagine. That's what I should have asked for, if I'd thought about it. I just really wanted hot pot."

"This way it'll be a good challenge for me, too."

I started getting the hot pot ready in the kitchen while Iwakura put on some music and read a book. Outside, the sky grew dark. The room got steamy, and every time I opened the rickety window to let the steam out, cold air rushed in and blew around the apartment.

We watched TV and filled our bellies with hot pot.

Time passed normally, and our conversation didn't turn romantic at all.

I may not have been a chef yet, but my kitchen training had taught me to clean up as I went, and Iwakura did most of the rest. After the hot pot, he made coffee and cut a cake roll that his mom had brought him. We were sitting at the *kotatsu* with our legs under the warm blanket. I had a thought.

"There's something unusual about this room. It feels peaceful, but also like time stops when you come through the door. It's so quiet compared to everywhere else, I feel like it calms me right down. I'm impressed you can live here and still find the energy to go to work. If it was me, I think I'd be tempted just to stay in."

Iwakura nodded.

"That's it. When I'm here my mind gets so quiet, it's like time stops. On top of that, it seems like there are other people here."

"Here in this building?" I asked, alarmed. I thought he might mean homeless people, or squatters.

"No, not like that. I mean . . . the landlords."

"They're still here?"

"What I mean is . . . it's kind of awkward. They're dead, but they don't seem to have noticed."

"What do you mean?"

"The two of them fell asleep with their brazier lit and died of carbon monoxide poisoning. The landlord and landlady. I mean, they were elderly, but still."

"In this room?"

"That's what happened . . ."

"You aren't telling me this hoping I'll get scared and jump into your arms so you can make a move, are you?"

"If only. But it's all true. Sometimes I see them here in the apartment."

I didn't know what to say.

"Are you . . . sensitive to that kind of thing?" I asked.

"Nope, not one bit. I spent the night in a grave-yard once, when I was traveling alone, and slept like a baby."

"Then how come . . ."

"Maybe because when I'm at home, I'm relaxed and have my guard down. Or I've just been working too hard. Anyway, every once in a while, when I'm just waking up, or when I come home tired and sit down with a cup of tea, it's like the two worlds intersect and I see them, still living here like they used to."

"Shouldn't you get the place cleansed, or something?"

"But the whole building's going to be gone soon. I don't think there's any harm in it," Iwakura said. "They look happy here."

This was precisely what made him so nice. He was even considerate to ghosts.

"Hmm," I said. I was skeptical. *Between worrying about his future and working too much, maybe he's starting to lose his grip. I should keep an eye on him*, I thought.

But the more pressing concern, for me, was how we were sitting across from each other at a kotatsu, steadily putting away a cake roll, and talking like this as though it were the most normal thing in the world. We seemed like an old couple ourselves, which struck me as pretty funny.

Afterward, he walked me back to my apartment, pushing his moped along so he could stop by the store on his way home.

"Secchan, why did you move out, when your family's only one train stop away?" he said.

It was a starry night, and the moon looked as sharp as ice. Its whiteness made it look like it had been cut out of the sky with scissors.

"My mom started hosting cooking lessons, for fun, and so many people started hanging around the house that I had to give up my room. But I treat this apartment like a bedroom. I still go home a lot, anyway. I'll eat dinner there and then come back here to sleep. I still help out at the restaurant a lot, too."

"That sounds nice. Like you're still in touch with the flow of things. I feel stranded right now."

"I have to make sure I keep some distance from them, though. Otherwise, everything becomes too close, and it takes away the time I need for myself. That's why I make a point of living on my own, and traveling, and things."

"That's what I thought. Maybe I got tired of it, too. Driving my parents out on trips and to the store, helping relatives move . . . I could just see a future where that was all I did. It's not that I mind, and it's not that I don't *want* to be a pastry chef, but still."

"You've got loads of time. Why don't you save up and get a job, or go study abroad for a while? You can't just be the dutiful child all the time, especially as a son. It makes you stingy, I think."

"That's it! My parents still see me on the same trajectory they pictured for me when I was a baby, but I've got my own life to live."

"Thanks for walking me home."

"Thanks for dinner. And sorry not to pay you back."

"Don't worry about it. The cake roll was delicious!"

Iwakura waved and rode off on his moped. It was old, but looked expensive, and had been lovingly maintained. *You can tell when people have been cared for,* I thought.

I could imagine how trying to save up money and leaving home would come with their own complications when you started with advantages like his. No wonder things seemed to be weighing on him.

In any case, the whole evening had been so remarkably ordinary, and my feelings so calm the entire time, that I decided then and there this would never develop into a romantic relationship—that we would just be friends.

"Mom, do you know an old apartment building near here where the landlords died of carbon monoxide poisoning?" I asked.

"I heard about it. It was on the news. I think they lit a brazier and fell asleep with the windows closed?"

"That's the one. Do you know anything else about them?"

My mom had grown up here, so I thought she might know the story.

We had closed and cleared the tables, and Mom and I were sitting at the counter eating our staff meal of crab pilaf and miso soup. The soup was Grandma's own recipe. If someone had told me that I'd been put on this earth solely to pass down the taste of this miso soup to future generations, I wouldn't have minded one bit. There was something almost magically inviting about it. Of course, Grandma had always made her miso paste from scratch.

"They used to come in often. Not so much once the gentleman started to have trouble walking, but weekday evenings, before the rush, they'd come in holding hands. Table six: omurice and pork curry. With side plates so they could share."

"Oh, I remember now. I can picture them."

"And a small bottle of beer. They were a cute old couple. You could tell their life was modest, but it seemed to be made up of all these little traditions they'd built up over the years. They were never a barrel of laughs or anything, but I always felt reassured when they came in. Dad and I used to say we wanted to be like them when we grew old. When we heard about what happened I remember telling him how—them going together in their sleep like that—maybe it was for the best," she said.

My parents were unbelievably devoted to each other.

Dad used to have a normal office job, but as a regular at the restaurant he fell in love with Mom and quit his job to learn to cook, and ended up running the place with her—a bold move for a respectable office worker. He always smiled and went along with whatever she wanted. I'd been against the cooking classes, but he'd said yes as soon as Mom had asked.

"For the love of God, please don't go together like them," I said.

"We're lucky the restaurant will be in good hands if we do," she said, and laughed.

This was a phrase she'd often directed at my brother when we were younger.

Mom always said it cheerfully and with the best of intentions, but each time she did, it landed somewhere inside my brother, and stuck. For him, it had become too much of a burden to bear.

I, on the other hand, had always envied him being the one she counted on.

Maybe on some level, my dream of taking on the restaurant came from a petty place—was just something I'd convinced myself of out of stubbornness. Perhaps I'd taken the feelings I had about my brother, not accepting what was being offered to him on a platter, perhaps I'd let them ferment into a kind of complex, and laid them on myself.

When my grandma died, though, it made me realize something.

At the funeral, middle-aged men whom Grandma had fed and counseled when they were young men turned up in black suits and told stories about times they brought their dates for meals at the restaurant, or how she comforted them with fried prawns when their girlfriends broke up with them.

For the first time, I saw the difference we made by being there for people over the years, in the background of their lives.

The utensils and fittings we handled every day took on deeper colors the more we used and polished them. In the same way, Grandma's life— which until then I'd only pictured as day after day at the same restaurant, serving the same dishes— suddenly seemed to have more depth than I could fathom.

I couldn't imagine anything in the world more meaningful than that.

For the next few weeks, Iwakura continued working long hours at the bar, and I kept busy with school, the restaurant, and my various hobbies.

At the restaurant we started serving the omu-rice on plates I'd made, so my pottery was becoming a useful and busy pursuit. I handwrote the menu board, so I had to keep up with calligraphy practice, too. My dedicated nature meant I was always looking for ways to make use of what I had. I couldn't really help it—that was just who I was, or at least what I was used to. The fact that I already knew what I would do after I finished college also meant I could put my energy into a variety of interests. My studies, on the other hand, could never have a practical application, so they never interested me much.

When I saw Iwakura around campus, I thought he looked a little washed out.

It had to be hard living on his own away from his family. I knew he was spending all his time either studying or working at the bar. He might have acted grown-up, but he was still a college student.

That said, I also thought that sharing a room inside a condemned building with a pair of ghosts couldn't help.

I felt uneasy. Ghosts probably lived in ghost time—time that flowed in its own strange way, somewhere completely removed from our own. Couldn't mixing in it, even just a little, sap you of some of the vitality you needed to live in this world?

Maybe I already liked Iwakura more than I realized.

About six months earlier, I'd broken up with someone I'd met at my pottery studio. It had been quite a major love affair. He was older and single, and I'd gotten caught up in it to the point that I'd even thought about marrying him. In the end we'd gone our separate ways, but I was still hung up on him. I didn't see him anymore because he'd gotten married to someone else and left the pottery class.

The woman my ex-boyfriend married was a co-worker who had initially approached him for advice about her relationship with her abusive husband.

My boyfriend had gotten drawn in and had come to feel he had to protect her.

With youth being my only asset, I'd been powerless to stop them being strongly drawn toward each other. I could only watch miserably from the sidelines.

Once, when things were slow at the bar, I'd mentioned the situation to Iwakura. I made light of it, like a joke. But he said, "A man who can get taken in by a move like that will never change. I'm glad you broke up."

I was pretty impressed that a boy of his age could have such an appropriate and reasonable opinion.

In fact, what he said continued to be a source of encouragement for me while I recovered from that tumultuous relationship. I never brought it up with Iwakura again, of course, and after a while I was able to put it all behind me, since my ex-boyfriend was married and no longer in my life. But Iwakura's calmness and his snub-nosed profile as he stood next to me polishing the glassware and told me what he thought stayed with me even after that.

●

That afternoon, I bumped into Iwakura at the station.

"How've you been?" I asked, smiling.

"I took your advice," he said promptly. "Are you free now? I'll tell you while we walk."

"Sure. I'm just on my way home," I said. "Are you working tonight?"

"Not tonight. But I've got to be up at six tomorrow," he said. I might have imagined it, but he seemed less pale and more alive than he had been lately.

"Seen any ghosts lately?" I asked.

"Yeah, sometimes. The old lady makes tea and folds laundry. The old man does stretches along to the radio."

"You moved out of your family's home into someone else's," I said. "I'm not sure that counts as living on your own."

"I'm used to it now. I hardly notice. Once in a while I'll see them and say hello. Even though it's not like they know I'm there."

It was a winter afternoon, and we were walking through the sparsely peopled streets.

Cars came and went, gleaming at one another in the low light, and the rows of plane trees along the street extended into the distance in their dull winter colors.

"So? What was this excellent advice you decided to take?" I asked.

"Going abroad. Only I've decided to go to patisserie school in Paris."

"But that's a cake-roll-track move!" I said.

"I realized I didn't want to end up as a cake baker who'd never been to France, you know?"

"I get it. I'd have done the same if we were an Italian restaurant. I'm lucky yoshoku is Japanese, so I don't need to go as far as you."

"I don't want to change what my old man's created in his cake roll, but I want a chance to figure out what it's all about for me separate from that, I guess. I might finish my training and get a job out there. I don't know yet. I'll need to see what happens, but right now that's what I'm leaning toward. It's not the working with my hands that I want to get away from, or the baking. Dessert gives people a moment to dream. It makes people happy. To start with, I was looking at schools in Japan, but the more I thought about it, the more I knew I wanted to go over there."

"Have you told your parents?"

"Yeah. They're dead against it."

"What are you going to do?"

"I have enough money to cover tuition, and to find a cheap apartment and support myself while I look for a job. I also have a savings account in my name. It's money my parents put away for me, so I'd rather not touch it, but still."

"Wow, Iwakura, that's great. You actually reached your goal."

"Yeah, well, I've really been cutting back," he said.

So he's leaving, I thought, and suddenly my chest gave a squeeze, and an unexpected loneliness settled over me. The sky above us looked sad and distant. Soon he'd go abroad and find his own world, and spend years over there, and maybe never come back.

I'd noticed already—though only vaguely, perhaps—that Iwakura wanted to sleep with me. There was something in his expression, his voice. A feeling of closeness lay silkily between us, like a sourdough starter quietly rising.

"I wish I could have tried your omurice, Secchan," Iwakura said. "I still regret asking you for hot pot that day. Even though it was delicious."

"Come to the restaurant and you can have it

anytime," I said. "I mean, it'll be my mom or dad cooking, but it'll taste pretty much the same. Mine's just a little less consistent than theirs."

"You've still got time to get it perfect," Iwakura said, and laughed.

"I can come over right now and make it for you," I said. "As long as you get the ingredients."

"Are you sure?"

"Uh-huh."

In that moment of melancholy, I think we both knew we might as well have been talking about having sex.

The cloudy winter sky felt unspeakably erotic, with its silvery hues and thickness of cloud, and the wind blowing through beneath. You could only think it was a setup designed to make you want to lay your skin against another's. It made me want to stay indoors under its grayness forever. With a stranger, in an apartment, luxuriating in unconstrained desire, the only place I felt like I could truly let go.

We stopped at the supermarket for ingredients, and then I was back in the run-down building's most haunted apartment.

This time around, there was nothing sinister about it at all. The room looked even more faded and see-through than before. The air was forsaken and crisp, and through the window, I saw clouds in heavy layers of gray, extending into the distance.

We talked about different things, occasionally opening the window to let out the heat of the cooking stove, and I made omurice. I couldn't have made a sauced dish away from home, but with omurice I could re-create more or less exactly how it would taste at the restaurant. For an extra treat I whipped up a miso soup with oysters to go with it.

It was a dish I could make with my eyes closed, one I'd long since had my fill of, but Iwakura seemed delighted. He even polished off my leftovers.

Each time he got up and went to the bathroom, I worried slightly that the ghosts would appear, but thankfully I remained the only one in the room, aside from the heating stove glowing yellow like an open fire.

Then it was eight o'clock and we were sitting at the kotatsu, talking about nothing in particular, digging into a fluffy cake roll with a slightly firm, caramelized surface and filled generously with whipped cream.

"How are you always in cake rolls here?"

"My mom brings them over, along with bags of rice."

"They must have enough food to feed the neighborhood, just like we do," I said. "I know the craze has passed, but you still can't say no to a cake roll."

"The fillings are seasonal. And they keep for a few days, so they're good for gifting. I think Japanese people just love cake rolls."

"What are the flavors just now?"

"Matcha, chestnut, and yuzu."

"Yuzu? I'm not sure I'd like that one."

How can I describe the unique relaxed feeling I had while Iwakura and I sat talking? He wasn't family, and it couldn't be described as fun. But something fell into place, and we could have talked forever, or been equally comfortable sitting in silence. Unlike when I was with other men, it never crossed my mind to worry about whether my makeup had rubbed off, or if my hair was sticking up.

"I think I'll get going," I said. "It's too bad I missed the ghosts."

"If you want to see them, you should spend the night," Iwakura said.

I was a little surprised. Only a little, admittedly.

"I don't want to see any ghosts, but what do you mean I should spend the night? Can you at least explain yourself?" I asked.

"Well," Iwakura said, and thought for a moment. He looked serious. "I guess when you work as a bartender, this kind of thing starts to seem like no big deal."

For obvious reasons, I was offended.

"Are you serious? You could at least pretend to be attracted to me, even though I know it's not true. Tell me that—if you had to say—you'd say I was pretty, or . . . There are so many things you could have said."

"If I had to, I'd say that out of all the girls I know, I like both the way you look and the way you are the best," Iwakura said.

He wouldn't have said it unless it was true. I felt a pang of pain in my chest.

"What I meant was that when you work at a bar and everyone our age goes out after finishing work, then you start asking people if they want to stay over without it meaning very much, and I've gotten so used to it that I don't feel those things so clearly anymore."

"That makes sense to me."

"And if you're a girl and you're at some guy's

31

apartment, you're testing the heat of the situation using your whole body. Or so I imagine."

"I think that's normal."

"But us guys, we only see holes. No matter how pretty a girl's makeup looks, or what she's wearing, or what ordinary thing we're talking about, all we can think of is how somewhere deep inside this person, there's a hole—a wet hole, and that's all we can see. Once the thought comes into your head, it's all there is."

"Okay?"

"So that's what's been on my mind. Every time you laugh or say anything, I'm still thinking about that hole."

"How am I supposed to feel about that? Flattered, or depressed?"

"Now that the thought's there, I can't stop myself from thinking about how I really want to do it. But I'm leaving the country soon, and I don't want any regrets."

"I know what you mean. We'll end up feeling sad no matter how we act on our desires right now. If we have sex, it'll probably make me start liking you."

"Same here. Even more than I like you already."

"It's bad timing."

"That's it."

"Well, maybe we can draw a line, and just agree to enjoy ourselves," I said. "There's no point thinking about the future. But I'm unattached, and there's a hole here."

"Are you sure?"

"Don't say that. Don't leave it up to me."

This is the strangest proposition I've ever received, I thought. *You're a funny one, Iwakura.*

I stayed the night at Iwakura's place.

I'd expected his futon to be flat and hard, but he was from a well-off family after all, and inside his closet there was an old but respectable mattress, a nice thick comforter, and clean sheets.

Outside, the cold wind blew and rattled at the windows.

That night, in the light of a small lamp, we had sex just once. We had incredibly sensual sex without either of us saying a word.

I'd only slept with one other man, but Iwakura's attention that night transformed my pleasure. He seemed to carefully inspect my body to find out where and how to touch me. He put aside his own arousal to do this, which made it even more exciting, and I orgasmed with another person for the first time ever. He saw it through, waited the proper length of time, and then entered me. It was a bizarre moment. We both felt as though we'd encountered sex for the first time, and it took our breath away. We could tell we were both wondering what it was we'd been thinking of as sex until then. Something just hard and slippery enough, somewhere just wet and tight enough—of course there could be nothing better. *So this is what sex is for*, I thought. *To experience the uniqueness and perfection of the way two people fit together.* No soreness or pain—only mutual enjoyment that stopped just when you wanted it to keep going forever, so you did it again. I understood this for the first time.

Afterward, we rolled ourselves up inside the comforter and lay together, close and warm.

Just before we fell asleep, Iwakura said, "This was what I really wanted. To sleep right next to someone like this, more than a hot pot."

"Maybe that's what it means to be young," I said. "You have a family to go home to, and they love you, but you feel lonely anyway." I was speaking from personal experience.

When I woke up, Iwakura had overslept and was trying to get dressed while brushing his teeth. He told me he had to go—could I lock the door and leave the key in the mailbox when I left?—and rushed off.

But before he did, he came and kissed me, still naked under the comforter, and said, "Let's see each other again before I leave."

Nestled under the covers, woozily giving myself over to the warmth of my own body, looking up at a gray sky that seemed to promise more snow, I fell back to sleep.

When I woke up again, I felt somber and alone, but also very satisfied. The time was 8 a.m.

Staying here and getting more comfortable in Iwakura's space will only make it harder, I thought, and told myself to get up. I had my own world to get back to, and my own life to start on.

I lit the gas stove to take the chill out of the room. I was gazing into its flames when I thought I sensed something move in the kitchen.

"I forgot about the ghosts," I said to myself.

I turned my head and saw the old woman at the sink with her back to me. Slowly, sedately, she was preparing water to make tea. It wasn't that the kettle moved, or that any water actually boiled. The half-transparent old woman simply made intermittent wavelike gestures that suggested that was what she was doing. Slowly, step by step, the usual motions, in the usual order, with the usual care, no doubt following a warm and comforting method that had been passed down from her mother, and her mother's mother before that.

I watched her for a while, remembering how my grandmother used to move like this in the kitchen, and feeling like a young child again. Whenever I was home sick with a fever, I used to watch her work. I felt like she'd bring me a bowl of rice porridge any moment now. It was a wistful, nostalgic, warm feeling.

In the next room, the old man was exercising along to the radio. He was dressed in a pair of light cotton trousers and completed each movement diligently, slowly unbending at the hips and knees. He must have thought this routine would keep his body fit for as long as he'd need it. He could hardly have known that the brazier would turn out to be their downfall.

The two of them would have lived modestly,

always greeted their tenants by name, collected everyone's rents regularly and noted them down in a ledger, and gone out once a month to the same restaurant to indulge modestly in the same meal.

Why, there's no need to be afraid of them. They don't mean to be dead. They'll simply keep on living the way they always did, forever.

My thoughts turned to Iwakura, under the covers here in this apartment, being with them quietly, keeping an eye on them, giving them space. I thought about his kind, parched heart, and thought I might be starting to have real feelings for him. My body, of course, still felt him everywhere. As weak, nice, and immature as he was, he was a man, and made love to me like one.

The old woman was still making small movements in the kitchen, and the old man was still doing his exercises. They looked intimate and peaceful, just like I remembered them from the restaurant.

I got dressed slowly so as not to disturb them, and quietly left the apartment.

At the door, I turned and said, "Thanks for having me."

But they took no notice, and carried on in their quiet existence.

•

Iwakura's plan was to get cheap language lessons until he left, from a French person he knew, and then enroll at a patisserie school just outside Paris once he could speak enough. So he became incredibly busy again, and even on the days when we did see each other at school, we'd only wave from afar, and before I knew it the day of his departure was nearly here.

I was vaguely avoiding him, wanting to put some distance between us.

I hadn't forgotten him saying, "Let's see each other again"—although it was more of a "let's do it again." I wanted to, of course. I think he did, too.

But I didn't call or message him.

I was trusting that the right opportunity would present itself.

And on the Friday morning exactly two weeks before his flight, a day of velvety gray clouds and a strong wind, we bumped into each other outside the train station.

We were in thick coats that seemed to draw attention to just how far we had come since summer, when we'd worked together at the bar.

"I'm going to skip my French lesson today. I should pack and get ready."

Iwakura was looking at me like someone in love. His gaze was hot, and I thought he might latch on to me right then and there. It wasn't a hungry look, but that of a man looking at something that was important to him.

"I'm going to skip work, too," I said. "But I want to stop by the bookstore."

We went to the bookstore, and then had lunch together.

"They're demolishing the apartment building. Just after I leave."

"What do you think will happen to them?"

"You saw them?"

"Yeah, they were just going about their day. It turns out they were regulars at the restaurant. I knew them. The man was stretching, and the woman was making tea."

"They seem harmless, don't they?"

"They actually made me feel pretty at home."

"Maybe we should light some incense for them, or something."

"I think so. I know we're not professionals, but it seems like the right thing to do."

We went and bought a single white chrysanthemum and some sticks of incense, as though we were the ones who were an old married couple. Then it came to me.

"What if we make them omurice and pork curry as an offering? I bet they must have missed having it."

Iwakura said he couldn't imagine anything more fitting, so we went to the supermarket for ingredients.

Walking shoulder to shoulder on a winter afternoon, dressed casually and holding bulky bags of groceries, anyone seeing us would have thought we were newlyweds, or a nice cohabiting couple. But we were only two people, a little regretful, and soon to part.

We were having so much fun that it made me sad.

Iwakura had already packed up most of his apartment. He told me he'd been offered a room with a family in return for babysitting their kids. His dad had gotten in touch with someone he knew over there.

"Does that mean he's changed his mind about you going?"

"My old man has. But my mom's still against it. I think she knows I might not come back. I don't want to lie, so I haven't promised them I will. I'll probably get my own place over there once I can afford it."

When he talked about the future, his face seemed to come alive. He looked like someone looking toward a world that was about to open up to him— almost like a different person from when he'd been working at the bar and trying to decide what to do after college. I could see in his eyes that training in France would serve him well. I felt happy for him, not jealous or regretful. I much preferred to see him like this, rather than the pale and tired version of Iwakura he'd been.

As soon as we were inside his apartment, Iwakura and I got under the comforter and had sex. Then, still naked, we talked for a while about different things—our hopes and worries, our families, our ideals, and our ambitions for the future.

The sadness hung around us the whole time. No matter what we were doing, the awareness that we'd soon be going our separate ways made me feel cold at the passing of time. Every laugh we shared was followed by a moment of sadness. But we were enjoying each other's company, so I tried to focus on the present.

When evening came and we got hungry, we found a sauté pan, a saucepan, a knife, and a cutting board from inside the moving boxes that were already packed, and I made pork curry and omurice.

I made the familiar dishes with as much care and attention as I could. The old couple had given my family the privilege of cooking the food that was the modest pleasure that garnished their final days, and the idea that I could offer some comfort to their spirits made me pour my heart into it. Never again would the two of them be able to come to the restaurant or taste their favorite meal. I just wanted to make sure they'd understand what I was trying to say with these dishes: *Thank you for coming to us all those years. It was an honor to do this for you.*

Most of the food was for Iwakura and me, but we plated up small portions on a paper plate and put them on the windowsill. We placed the chrysanthemum in a paper cup next to it, lit some incense, then put our palms together and prayed for their spirits to move on when the building was torn down. We left them a small bottle of beer, too.

I felt then that I'd done everything I could. It was a light, spacious feeling.

Giving back to those who knew and loved my family's food—this was another part of my calling.

Just like last time, Iwakura ate up what I had cooked and said it was delicious.

Then, a little more calmly this time, we had sex again.

"It seems like a shame to be apart, when this is getting even better," Iwakura said. I felt the same.

The ghosts didn't show. They must have been satisfied with their meal.

I decided to leave later that night, because I knew staying would make me too sad. Iwakura walked me home.

There was something lighter about the two of us as we made our way through the dark streets.

"I'll write you emails."

"Good. I had a great time. Thanks."

We smiled, and embraced. The heat of our bodies inside our coats joined together, and we were very warm.

"It seems strange to be saying goodbye when we like each other so much," I said, and when I looked up I saw there were tears in Iwakura's eyes, too.

"We were both too nice to sleep together and keep things casual."

"The whole point of you leaving the country is so you can stop being so nice, remember?"

"Yeah, but it's too late with you. You've seen everything."

"Well, if we ever get another chance, then."

And that was how we left things.

Iwakura stood there in the street in the dark and watched me leave, waving, and waving.

I think it was out of care for one another's futures that we both stopped contacting each other.

Iwakura emailed me exactly once. Along with a general update, he said:

"No one seems to find me attractive over here."

The tone of it, the way it seemed to miss the point, brought him back to me so vividly it made me want to weep.

Iwakura standing and looking slightly lost like he always did; the colors of all the skies we looked up at together; the way his hands and fingers had felt on my skin—all of him came back to me in a rush.

There was only one thing stopping us from being really good together, I thought. *But now we'll never see each other again.* And the tears were rolling down my cheeks.

Not long after that, I happened to walk past Iwakura's old block. His building was completely gone, and there was a brand-new apartment building in its place. This, too, was part of my job—to bear witness to the changing of the neighborhood—but this time I felt the loss in my heart. Our hot feelings were now buried firmly in the past, just like the old couple.

May all that lingers find peace, I thought as I walked away.

And sure enough, with the passing of time, I forgot it all.

But then—somehow, eight years later, we'd be married.

Fate had to have something to do with it.

Before that, though, Iwakura spent eight years as a patissier at a restaurant on the outskirts of Paris. I assume, of course, that in that time there were many love affairs, and the joys and sorrows that come with them.

For my part, I fell in love and considered giving

up the restaurant to be his wife, but in the end, we went our separate ways and I returned to my calling. It would be a while yet before I was truly in charge at the restaurant, but I could keep the place running for a week while my parents went off to relax at a hot spring.

Iwakura's mother passed away from a heart attack last April.

I didn't go to the funeral. I didn't want to impose on the family simply because I'd slept with their son a few times. So in my mind I sent my condolences, and briefly wondered whether Iwakura had come back, but over the years my memories of him had faded along with the rest of my carefree college days, so I didn't particularly hope to see him.

Part of the reason was that several of our regulars had expressed their interest in me, and thanks to my parents giving me a role as the face of the restaurant, I had my pick from among them, and was just then on the verge of developing something good with one.

The person was training to be a chef, so our plans for the future were compatible. He was big and kind and reminded me of my grandpa, and at the time I was envisioning a future where the two of us would be married.

But that was just when Iwakura and I happened to meet again. Perhaps it wasn't so unexpected, since we were in our hometown, but the two of us seemed fated to keep meeting at moments when we had unexpected pockets of freedom in our usually full lives.

I was in a café near home, having a cup of tea, when he came through the door.

I noticed the sophisticated colors of his clothing before I noticed it was him.

He seemed as surprised to see me as I was to see him, but I waved him over and he came and sat down across from me.

I noticed how living abroad for so long had changed the texture of his skin. His right arm had grown strong from making all that pastry, and his shoulders were much more solid than before, and his face narrower, like it had been pared down. His eyes, which had been so soft and kind before, were now the sharp eyes of a man who knew both loneliness and independence.

So this was who he wanted to be, I thought, *the*

person he had to go abroad to become. Now that he was in front of me, it all made sense. I finally saw it. From what he had told me back then, I hadn't understood what he was looking for.

His smile still lit up his face just like it had before.

"How long has it been? You look all older," I said.

"You're not so bad yourself," he said, and smiled.

Our table was bathed in the light of early summer streaming through the window next to it, and outside, on the corner, people leaving the train station turned onto the side streets of the neighborhood with freshly uncovered arms almost too dazzling to look at. The branches of the trees along the street were reaching upward toward the sky.

"I've come back to run the bakery."

"I thought you would," I said.

I knew that with his mom gone, there was no way he'd have left his dad to manage the bakery alone.

"Your mom—did you get to see her?"

"Yeah. When she had her first attack, I was here for a month. I visited her every day in hospital, and we took her to a hot spring once she was discharged. She didn't say a word to me about the bakery. She was just happy to spend some time together. So that gave me some things to think about. It wasn't the easiest decision, but there isn't as much keeping me in France now—the restaurant just expanded and took on new chefs, but I've more or less finished training them, so they'll be all right. It seemed like the right time for a change."

"How's your dad doing?"

"He's taken it really hard. It's tough to see him like this."

"What's going to happen with the bakery? Your dad on cake rolls, you doing other cakes?"

"I thought about it, but our cake rolls are what we're known for, so I'm going to keep my other pastries for Christmas or special orders. Now that I know better, I can see there's something to the old man's methods and techniques. I mean, all that training, and I still can't bake a better cake roll."

"Do you think you could?"

"I might, if I keep learning from him. He's a real artist—he tells me the sponge is done when it's moist, but not hot to the touch; or the batter's different every day, but not because of the temperature or the weather, but because of something he can't explain! And he always knows just when to add the oil to the mix, and how much. I used to think his opinions were just things he'd cobbled together to make up for not having had the proper training, but in Paris, I learned a lot more from the ways things were done at each place I worked than I ever did at school. So I started to think about what my old man says in the same way. Who knows? Maybe my work will be to carry on what he's created with his cake rolls. I want to understand how he does it and make it mine. But I'll bake other things, too. He seems to like it when I show him things I've picked up. Maybe we'll come up with some new cakes together. He'd like that."

"How will the store carry on without your mom?"

"It's a concern. People loved buying cakes from her. Now that it's just the two of us, we can change a few things, maybe go with a slightly more plainspoken tone. It might take some time, but— we couldn't do it her way even if we stood on our heads. Hers was a real gift. But I learned a lot while I was over there about valuing your traditions and your elders and your relationships, and that opened my eyes a little. And now that I can see myself as an equal with the old man, that means I can pull my weight, too. I even learned to cook some French food."

"Please don't tell me you're going to open a French restaurant and compete with us, Iwakura. Times are hard enough already."

"I didn't say I was good. Anyway, your place is doing okay, isn't it?"

"The old regulars are so picky about the taste. When I'm the only one in the kitchen, some of them let me know just how much further I've got to go."

"Well, I know you've got nothing to worry about there, Secchan."

We were speaking familiarly now, and it felt bittersweet.

And then, suddenly, time was flowing differently than usual.

It didn't turn back, or even pause.

Time simply floated open and started to expand. Time held the two of us in light, inside a space so vast it might have reached the heavens, and turned eternal.

I assumed this experience was something personal and internal to me, but when I asked Iwakura later, he'd had the exact same feeling.

Just then, of course, there wasn't even a hint of sexual desire between us.

In the window where we drank tea, the light

fell and covered us in a buoyant, warm yellow glow. It was a light we'd been waiting for—that told our parched hearts this was what had been missing.

The best words I can find to describe it is to say I felt we were being blessed.

It was the feeling of finally finding what we'd been looking for after so long.

Because we'd been so young before, I'd assumed it had been the sex that connected us, but I was wrong. Just talking casually together like this made an indescribable aliveness come bubbling up from deep inside me, and I recognized it, and knew it was right.

The feeling turned into certainty, and the two of us sat there smiling and satisfied. This time we were in now would never end, we thought. This was it. We'd known something was missing, felt that something had been lost. Deep in our hearts we knew what it was, but we never suspected it was this. My soul spoke, and what it said was: *We've been lonely for so long, and this was why. We were so lonely we couldn't even know it.*

The lights inside us both, the clean and clear light outside, and the light that now glowed between us all joined together as one, and lit the way to the future.

We exchanged numbers, and a week later, Iwakura called and said, "If you're single, let's get married."

I'd been thinking the same, so I immediately agreed. "I'm unattached just now, and there's a hole here."

At the other end of the line, Iwakura burst out laughing.

We made arrangements for the marriage quickly, on the understanding that each of us would continue running our respective family business. My parents were a little surprised, but they soon came around to the idea.

The only changes we would be making at the restaurant would be to hire a professional chef—not the one who was in love with me—to assist me so I could have more of a family life, and to add cake rolls to the menu.

I carefully wrote "Cake roll of the week ¥600" on the menu board, and we started serving them up on dessert plates I'd made, two thick slices to a serving.

Over the years, I'd often found myself frustrated by quite how long things always seemed to take me. But I kept at it, and tried to accept myself for who I was, and be happy with the life that came with it.

In the end, that turned out to be far less boring than I expected.

When Iwakura said, out of nowhere, "I almost wish we could invite them to the wedding," I nodded immediately, because I knew exactly who he had in mind. The unfurnished apartment had reminded me of them, too.

We'd decided on Nice for our honeymoon. Since Iwakura spoke French, I couldn't have been any more excited. He knew all the restaurants and hotels we'd visit. And just like that, my world, which had been so small, got a little bigger. Then we started looking for a place to live, and after a long search, we found the right apartment.

We'd popped in to take measurements for the curtains ahead of moving in.

Iwakura said, "I don't think we'll have any ghosts here."

The last eight years had changed him completely,

apart from the ways in which he hadn't changed at all.

His jackets, which were of a cut that no one in Japan owned, the patisserie tools he'd brought back, hearing him speak French on international calls— all of these actually filled me with hope.

I welcomed these new things coming into my life.

I sometimes worried if he found it boring being with me. I'd always been right here, doing this. The only things I contributed to his life were the unenviable position of having a wife who had her own business, and my omurice. I was convinced he'd rather be with someone who was good with customers, like his mom, or someone with a more impressive or sophisticated career.

I asked him about it a few times, but he said he didn't find me boring at all, that he liked how he felt at ease with me, and that both my face and my body were more attractive to him now than when we first met.

Admittedly, my body had changed from my unripe, sticklike, girlish figure into a womanly shape. Sometimes when I looked at myself in the bathroom mirror, I noticed the curves of my own waist and thought it was sexy. My bottom was solid, my ankles narrow, and my breasts were round with soft pink nipples. I looked good. It was another benefit of having an active job.

"That old couple—do you think they were able to move on?"

"The omurice and the curry will have done the job, I'm sure of it. Didn't you say they stopped being able to come to the restaurant toward the end, because of the old man's leg?"

"That's what my mom said. I guess they would have enjoyed it." I smiled.

I might never get another chance to cook a meal as powerful as that one, but even now, when I got tired and my arms felt heavy, or I started to overseason my dishes, I could think back to the intention I'd poured into it—the old couple's final supper on earth, and my last send-off for Iwakura—and remind myself what it was all for.

Being a cook meant any meal I made could end up being someone's last.

"Once we settle in, I'm thinking of starting a delivery service for old folks living alone in the neighborhood. Put together a cheap omurice bento or something," I said.

"I want to do something similar. In France, especially outside of Paris, all the shops, even the small-
est boulangerie, are there primarily to serve the
community. Customers who come from far away
are important, too, but there's real pride in main-
taining the quality of local life," Iwakura said. "Let's
find a way to combine the restaurant and the bakery
someday."

"I'd love to find a bigger lot, so we can live
there, too."

But until then, this apartment would be our
home.

The room was sunny and airy, and it had a view
of the trees in the park, and the happy voices of
children drifted over from the nearby elementary
school. It was very different from Iwakura's old run-
down apartment. We were older now, and there were
probably no ghosts here.

We'd needed to be apart, and grow older and
wiser, to arrve at that moment of realization when
we understood that the simple time we shared—
sitting in a warm kotatsu with someone close to
you, talking, or being together in silence, maybe
feeling impressed sometimes, or at other times a little bored, never getting irritated or pushy—was far

more important than fighting and then making up again passionately, or sex.

To feel that the latter was important, in itself, now seemed like youth. That must have been why neither of us had seen the other's value back then. At the same time, we must have known it somewhere to have been able to recognize it years later.

That said, I knew that for us, even as we'd go on to busy ourselves in our daily lives, the existence of a "hole" and a "pole" would remain—unbeknownst to others—at the core of our relationship. And we'd spend our nights holding forth on unimportant topics, or having sex, and grow old together. We'd nurture our connection, which was neither simply physical nor solely emotional, and that would expand the space that belonged to just the two of us until there was no escaping it.

We'd travel first to Nice and then to many other places, and find out just how sexually compatible we were.

But we'd never have better than that time, under the cloudy sky, wrapped in the comforter, in the warm room inhabited by ghosts.

The feeling we found then would always be the foundation of our relationship.

And someday we'd disappear like that old couple, leaving barely a trace.

This life seemed simple at first glace, when in fact it existed within a flow that was far bigger, as vast as the seven seas. My dead grandma was part of it now, and Iwakura's mom. The old couple, too. All of them had lived within that flow, and though each of us might strive or struggle against the current, we were all, in the end, part of the same water.

My only question is: What if—just if—I hadn't seen the old couple in Iwakura's apartment that day? Would he and I be married now?

Somehow, I think the answer is no.

It's only a hunch, but I'm pretty sure it's true.

"Mama!"

It was lunch, and my only concern was the menu on the wall outside the staff cafeteria.

Soba noodle soup. Fried shrimp combo. Vegetable curry.

I was pretty hungry.

I stood in front of the whiteboard for a moment and thought about which to go for.

Vegetable curry, I decided, and for a split second the Wakayama curry poisoning case crossed my mind. I remember that clearly.

Maybe it was my intuition talking. Just the day before, I'd watched a TV special about the housewife who'd put arsenic in the curry at a local festival. Whatever it was, I should have listened and stopped there.

But it seems unlikely that little flash of intuition

would have been enough to keep me from what I was about to do. I was on the cusp of getting pulled into a cascade of events that was already waiting to unfold.

I've never really thought of it this way before, but I think now that what I went through was fated to happen. Different things came together, threads that were far apart suddenly joined up, and circumstances reeled me in, smoothly and inescapably. I certainly hadn't been looking for a change.

All I was thinking was *I'm starving.*

I didn't feel like fritters or even noodles would hit the spot. *If only the soba still came with duck like it did last week*, I thought, and headed into the staff cafeteria.

Just as I walked in, a man came out, and we collided slightly. He was middle-aged and shabby-looking with messy hair, wearing dark clothing with no jacket. His eyes were cast down, and we passed each other in a second, so I couldn't tell who it was at all.

I learned later it was Mr. Yamazoe, a colleague I knew who used to work in another editorial group on the same floor as me.

I didn't recognize him at all.

I'd been busy and had taken my lunch later than usual, so I'd missed Mitsuko. She worked in the admin department and was my closest friend at work. We always sat together and talked over lunch when we could.

The cafeteria was as empty as I'd ever seen it, and most of the people there were slowly finishing up. Fewer than half the tables were occupied, so I hesitated for a second and then put my files down on a table by a window. Outside, I could see the parking lot, and mounds of fallen ginkgo leaves under the trees. With my wallet in my hand, I stood up to go and get the curry and some tea.

I bought a food token and handed it in at the counter. The kindly woman in the white chef's jacket smiled and said, "One curry, coming up," and went into the kitchen.

I went to the tea machine and got a cup of tea, then went back to the counter to collect my curry.

I remember thinking to myself how comforting it felt to do things step by step like this. The satisfaction of a meal coming together, one element at a time. *That's the joy of lunchtime*, I was thinking, without a care in the world, practically ready to start humming a tune.

In hindsight, I wonder whether God gave me that moment of feeling good out of pity for me for what was about to happen.

There was a delicious feeling of warmth in my chest that made me feel like something good was just around the corner.

That couldn't have been further from the truth, but when I think about that last moment of blissful ignorance, I almost feel like chuckling fondly.

No one saw me in that moment.

Each of the few people there was busy with their own thoughts, or the conversation at their table, and none of them noticed anything out of the ordinary.

I went back to my seat and started eating in silence while looking through my work.

Unluckily, I'd had a bad cold the previous week and still had a sore throat. On top of that, the afternoon sun coming in through the window was hot and bright, and I was feeling a little distracted.

The document I was looking at was the proof of a book. Soon I was too focused on my work to consider how the curry tasted, and I was simply chewing and swallowing each mouthful like a goat. What was more, the cafeteria curry was always strongly spiced, so I just thought that the hint of bitterness I sensed was how it was supposed to taste that day.

Then ... later that afternoon, I started to feel nauseated. I got up from my desk and went to the ladies' room to vomit, but that didn't relieve the sick feeling, and in the end I vomited repeatedly until I became so dehydrated that I lost consciousness and collapsed in the ladies' room, and my boss had to drive me to the large emergency hospital near the publishing company where I worked.

"Poor you!"

The next day, when Mitsuko came to visit, I was feeling perfectly fine, and was sitting up in bed going through the rest of the proof I'd been looking at the day before.

The author whose proof I was going over had sent flowers. On the card, it said: "What a calamity! So glad you're okay. Take as long as you need to recover—don't worry about my book."

Thanks, but the company might feel differently about that, I'd thought. And finding it easier to keep busy, I'd found myself reaching for my work again while I was still in the hospital.

Partly I was still taking my health for granted, but I was also loath to let something like this get in the way of my work.

I smiled and said, "I don't know how I'm going to face going back to the office after the whole floor heard me groaning and throwing up. I didn't think of this until now, but what am I going to tell people? And I can't believe they had my picture on the news. I think I might cry."

"The whole company knows," Mitsuko said, and laughed. "Everyone's talking about you. You could probably take your pick of the men in the office right now."

"I've got a boyfriend, I'm not interested. Although I admit it was exciting when the president visited yesterday. I felt like Cinderella," I said, and laughed.

"He's divorced and single right now, and still pretty hot at his age."

"Yeah, he came in looking so elegant, it was like spring suddenly burst into this drab room, you know? Of course he'd brought flowers and everything, him and his secretary Mr. Tanaka. I never thought he'd come in person. And there I was in a rumpled hospital gown with a drip in my arm—I almost felt like I should be apologizing."

"Yeah, but you got poisoned in the staff cafeteria! It's only right he came," Mitsuko said, looking indignant. "They said you were the last one to have the curry, since lunch was almost over."

"Thank God I was the only victim. It was awful—I really thought I was going to die. I had no idea what was happening to me."

"What a disaster. That guy Yamazoe—did you hear about how he was stalking the young writer he used to work with, after he got reassigned? It was maybe a year ago. Showing up to her home at night, harassing her with phone calls, following her around, the whole nine yards. And then when he got fired, he turned around and started targeting the company. Apparently he was even seeing a psychiatrist. He kept hounding the company claiming that he was owed royalties for cowriting her bestseller. So the company paid for her to relocate. I even heard her new editor had to be her security detail for a while. Everyone in that department knew, but the section head told them to keep it under wraps."

"I think I'd have done the same, in that position. You'd never dream things could turn out like this. I used to see Mr. Yamazoe around before he left. He always looked neat, and like he was good at his job, so I didn't recognize him in the cafeteria. I thought he was someone from publicity who'd been on an all-nighter or something. But I guess it was lucky for me that he let himself be caught so quickly, so they knew what the poison was and how to treat it. That's what the doctors said.

"It's a pretty terrible thing for him to have done, but when I think of how wretched he looked when we passed each other, I can't find it in myself to blame him too much. He seemed like a completely different person."

That was my honest truth.

In that moment, I could vividly recall Mr. Yamazoe's downtrodden, desperate manner, like he had nowhere left to go, when once he had blended in at the office, and looked like he belonged there.

He'd had the air of someone going down a road on which there was no turning back.

No doubt he'd never expected to end up there, either.

Maybe it was true that he and the writer had been lovers. Even if he hadn't coauthored her book, he'd probably read her work and offered advice.

Maybe their relationship just happened to set off

something deep inside him, so that he'd gradually strayed farther and farther away from what he intended, until he lost control.

"The problem with you, Matsuoka, is you're too understanding." Mitsuko laughed. "You basically got mixed up in some relationship drama, except these are people you barely know, who put your actual life in danger! You should be more angry."

"Honestly, I never thought something like this would happen to me. I thought it was the kind of thing that happens to other people. I still can't believe I'm really lying in this bed with a needle in my arm," I said. It was where I was at that moment. Never mind feeling angry, I was still trying to wrap my head around what on earth had happened.

Mitsuko nodded and said seriously, "Of course, quite a few people have fallen apart and quit recently. But I didn't think Mr. Yamazoe would be the type to stalk anyone, let alone poison the cafeteria curry. I couldn't have imagined anything like that would happen to us. Did you hear the writer he stalked was on TV in tears, sending you her apologies? Seriously, what a thing to get mixed up in! Anyway, I'm just relieved you're okay.

"Think about it—if the poison had been something

stronger, you'd be a goner by now. And then I'd prob-ably have been so shocked and lonely that I'd have had to quit. It scares me just thinking that you, and other people, could have died from this."

I found Mitsuko's sincerity grounding some-how. She made me want to be back at work already, picking up my life where I'd left it.

"I'm not eating in the cafeteria for a while," I said and laughed.

"No, how could you? I hear loads of people are avoiding it," she said. "I feel bad for the lunch lady."

"Really? In that case, I'll go," I said. "What are the chances of something like this happening again?"

"Okay, but if you ever feel iffy about it, come get me. I'm always taking lunch at weird hours, so I can join you anytime. We can go out to eat somewhere," Mitsuko said, taking my hand.

"Thanks." I was grateful for her thoughtfulness.

But at that point, I was still charged up from the urgency of the incident and being rushed to the hospital, and what with everyone including the company president giving me attention for be-ing the victim of terrible misfortune, the speed at which things had happened, the knowledge that I'd survived, and the relief of being in the hospital, I was yet to understand how much damage had been done to my liver, and the effect it was going to have on my future.

The poison that Mr. Yamazoe had mixed into the curry was a massive amount of cold and flu medicine.

The doctors pumped my stomach, ran test after test, and kept me hooked up to an IV the whole time. After five days, they told me: *No alcohol, no strenuous exercise, no stress, no strongly spiced food, no medication except the drugs we give you, plenty of rest, and come back for more tests. If you notice any changes in your mood, we'll refer you for counseling immediately, so just let us know.*

I hadn't noticed it while I was still in the hospital, but when I looked at myself in the mirror my color was very off, and I felt incredibly lethargic.

What was this feeling? I didn't know how to describe it. I just felt leaden, like something was weighing on me inside and bringing me very low. It was as if energy just drained straight out of my body without my doing anything at all, leaving me wrung out like a dripping rag.

But I hated to be in bed at home while people

were talking about me, and it wasn't like I couldn't get up, so I went in to the office as usual. I didn't want people thinking I was struggling to cope.

Truthfully, it felt like it took all my energy just to get on the train and reach the office, but I got through my work in spite of the intractable tiredness and lack of enthusiasm, and because I had to watch what I ate and drank, I could beg off dinner meetings and leave early, and I could keep most of my heaviness hidden.

At first, people watched over me with curiosity, and came and asked all kinds of questions, or nudged one another and said, *It's her—the one that got poisoned . . .* or *She looks much better than when I saw them take her away,* when they saw me in the hallway or in the bathroom. It was mortifying, but time soon passed. I felt like the view outside had changed while I was still up to my neck in a swimming pool of exhaustion.

When I decided to be brave for the sake of the lunch lady, went to the cafeteria with Mitsuko, and had the duck soba, people gave me a round of applause.

"Mama!"

This all built up the idea that I'd recovered, and people gradually stopped paying attention to me. So things around me returned to their regular, peaceful flow.

Leaving behind something inside me, which had been triggered without my even knowing.

In hindsight, though, I can see that—though I'd blamed it on the heaviness at the time—I'd felt irritated whenever I had to answer questions from the police or doctors.

The anger would rise, making me want to lash out and yell, "Just leave me alone!"

Yu, my boyfriend, had to bear the brunt of it.

Yu and I had been together for over three years, and we were living together as a trial before getting married. So my colleagues had his phone number, and he rushed to the hospital as soon as he heard. He was also the one who contacted my grandparents, who had brought me up.

He left work early and stuck by my bedside after I had my stomach pumped and got asked a bunch of questions by different people.

I'd been so relieved to see him when he arrived.

I'd be even happier if only I didn't feel so heavy, I thought.

Now that we were living together, he really was my closest family.

Everyone spoiled me for the next few days. Yu said, *Hospital food can't be the best*, and asked his mom to make tasty soft congee, which he would bring to the hospital and warm up in the microwave. He and my grandma got to know each other much better from interacting every time she went to pick up clothes and other things I asked for. In my bed at the hospital, I felt that my loved ones were always around me.

Through my heaviness, I thought, *My family's growing*, and that happiness warmed me gently. These were the bonds that grew stronger in unforeseen circumstances.

Each time I saw my family blaming Mr. Yamazoe or the company, or getting angry or crying for me, it made me think, hesitantly, that this was how it felt to be loved.

"I'm sorry. I didn't really understand that your parents weren't around," Yu said simply, one night when he'd snuck in long after visiting hours and brought me apples. We were watching TV with the volume turned down. In his hands an apple was turning around and around, being peeled smoothly.

The company had gotten me a private room, so the nurses were pretty lenient when it came to visitors.

The stillness of the hospital at night made it seem like Yu and I were the only two people in the world. Our voices naturally became quiet, too, and we were in a small, hushed place we'd never been in before.

I was feeling a little depressed again that night, because of my body feeling so heavy and not being able to move as I wanted it to. I felt stuck mentally, too.

I ate the crisp apple he'd peeled for me without saying anything. Just for a second, I felt refreshed by its sourness and sweetness, but in the state I was in, sitting up was still exhausting. The IV needle bothered me more each day, and the tape that held it itched, and my back hurt from lying in bed too long.

Basically, even if I loved him, and even if we'd been together a long time, telling him about something serious like this was the last thing I had the energy for just then.

"I was able to have a long conversation with your grandma the other day, and she told me a lot of things I didn't know. I feel bad that I never asked you about it," he said.

"Stop it. Don't talk like that," I said, and it came out harsher than I'd intended. My cranky voice echoed in the quiet room. The irritation came bubbling up like a spring from the pit of my stomach, and I had to stop it from exploding.

As it turned out, it was the apple that stopped me.

Its neat red peel lay curled on a plate. Yu had gone out of his way after a long day at work to visit me, and even peeled me an apple, and his surprised expression at the vehemence of my words looked like the apple, which simply existed there, innocent and beautiful.

With an effort, I went on a little more calmly.

"It's not like I even remember most of it. And I know you've been through a lot too, with your dad dying and your mom getting remarried, but those are things you can talk about but never fully describe, aren't they? So it's not that different from you not talking about those things," I said, and continued: "I'm not feeling great right now, but I'm going to get better. And since I hope to be making my own home soon, I can't really think about the past right now. Sure, I might have some emotional scars, but I don't think I've tried to ignore them, and of course, I might not be completely over what happened, since I was so young I don't remember it clearly, but Grandma and Grandpa truly loved me like I was their own child, so I haven't lacked for love. I don't have any hidden twists in my heart. You have nothing to worry about."

"I've been with you long enough to know that. And your grandparents are great," he said. "But something like this happens and suddenly people are talking about it, asking you things. It must be upsetting."

It was just like him to be so perceptive. Normally he was pretty happy-go-lucky, and not very interested in having serious conversations, but he noticed a lot when it came to people's expressions and tone of voice.

"Yeah. Maybe there's some of that. I think I'll feel calmer once people start moving on," I said.

"You know, I was kind of worried, because you've been looking pretty down since it happened. But I guess no one in the world's going to look contented after nearly being murdered," he said and smiled.

He was right that whenever I talked about my parents, my family, or memories growing up and things like that, I always felt the world around me get a little darker, like some heavy lump was forming somewhere inside me. But it always disappeared quickly once I stopped.

I was living in the present now, and I had my job, and I'd started my life together with my boyfriend, who had a tranquil and noble soul, and with whom I got along so well.

When I was surrounded by romance-obsessed pubescent classmates in high school, or marriage-obsessed colleagues when I first started working, I'd always stayed true to my inner world and protected it.

Somewhere in my heart, I'd been envious of everyone else.

I'd thought that people who liked to get carried away with romance were people who could afford to be careless with love—the kind of love you could let run freely and then drain away, like city water from a faucet.

There would be exceptions, of course, but that was how the people around me who were interested in relationships looked to me. *That must be nice,* I thought, *to be able to be so carefree with the love you have.*

I'd never doubted my grandparents' love, but there was the sense that I owed them for having taken me in. Like I was renting a room in the home of people I adored, I was always aware that I could behave like a spoiled child to the extent that it made them happy, but I couldn't afford to be too much trouble.

I was also learning that every single person in the world had been hurt by their family at some point. I wasn't special at all—some people dealt with it well, and some didn't, but that was the only difference, and either way, we were all nourished and cherished by our families, and at the same time limited and defined by them—that was what it meant to be human, I understood.

So I was cautious about starting a family of my own. Yu had wanted to get married straightaway, but I'd said we should live together for a year before making a decision.

I was nearly thirty, and I'd only ever been with three men, in serious relationships that had nothing at all to do with cheating or affairs.

Yu and I worked better than I'd expected once

we lived together. We had similar food preferences, and when it came to sharing housework we seemed to find a natural spaciousness and rhythm, perhaps because he'd lived alone with his mother for so long. On Saturday nights we always had sex and took a bath together afterward. Then we'd gaze into each other's eyes, and fall asleep smiling.

Our relationship felt so much more stable and easy than when we'd just been dating, which astonished me.

I'd started to think maybe this was the life I'd been looking for all along. The kind of life that needed no justification, where I felt calm and grounded, and which I would have been content to continue with forever.

Maybe all those people I'd thought treated love so carelessly never had to cling to things because they'd always lived with this kind of safety. And maybe this meant I could now start to become more and more like them. I'd always felt slightly intimidated by the idea of getting married or having children, but maybe it was nothing to be afraid of. I was starting to feel quite optimistic about things to come.

So the curry incident befell me just at the moment when the inexplicable nervousness that had blanketed me—the exact feeling that had made all the men before Yu distance themselves eventually—was just beginning to loosen the hold it had had over my life for so long.

As for my outburst in the hospital room that night, I assumed afterward that I'd simply been feeling a little needy, and forgot all about it.

One night, when I was close to being discharged, I found myself having trouble getting to sleep. Although I had finally been freed from the IV, the place where the adhesive bandage had held the needle itched and kept me awake. I got so bored that I went out in the middle of the night to the courtyard. The hospital at night was terribly quiet, and as I looked up, the giant building I had just emerged from loomed over me, with its dark windows and its bright windows making a pattern in the gloom.

I stood gazing up at it in my hospital gown.

Beyond the building, so many distant stars were blinking.

Each one of us inside this building is facing a threat to their life, I thought. *I got lucky and made it, and that's the only reason I'm out here feeling bored right now, breathing deeply in this fresh air, walking on my own two legs. But many of us won't leave the hospital alive.*

And yet it's all so quiet.

I felt the silence might swallow me up, that I might disappear inside it.

When I remember how small I felt then, it still makes me feel lonely.

My small back, small hands, small feet. With my heart and body so weak I could only walk at a snail's pace. I was doing my best to look out into space, but I felt so frail, I thought I might be blown away by a gust of wind.

In that moment, something so enormous and fundamental that I normally forgot its existence amid daily things and loved ones and life was trying to crush me along with the quietness. In my ignorance of what was about to happen, I went out into the darkness, defenselessly. To be shown just how small I was.

Soon after, I was discharged from the hospital and went back to work.

All I had to do now was get back to how I'd been physically, and everything would be just as it had been . . . or so I thought. Having never experienced serious illness before, I imagined that recovery would arrive suddenly and completely some fine morning. Like when you caught a cold, ran a fever, sweated through the night, and woke up the next morning with your fever gone and your head clear—that was how I thought it worked.

I didn't know that recovery was a process, like peeling back layers of tracing paper, and taking steps forward and then back, so I was internally starting to feel pretty anxious. It dawned on me that because I'd never spent much time in hospitals before, the scenes and impressions the place gave me when I went back for checkups reminded me of the past, and only increased my feelings of depression and lethargy, but there was nothing I could do about that while the world around me moved forward with forgetting about the whole incident altogether.

When our days off coincided, Yu did his best to be kind to me, and would take me out on scenic drives.

He knew that was the thing I enjoyed most.

But even getting in the car made me feel sick, and taking a sip of water made me nauseated. Even without that, the whole world looked one step darker, and the pressure of the landscapes that appeared rapidly before my eyes out of that darkness overwhelmed me.

The vibrant greens and the ocean waves were too vivid, too bright for me in my weakened state, and I was suffering.

This is all so pretty. It's beautiful. But I just want to get home and get under the covers. I'm not sleepy, but I've spent so long in bright light that I want to go to sleep.

I could barely eat anything good, and I'd lost too much weight to keep my strength up, and when I walked my legs were heavy, and I felt as though I had to drag them along.

But it wasn't as though I couldn't keep up if I really tried, so I never mentioned this heaviness to Yu, who was being so considerate of me.

Will I ever feel better enough to take in the power of these wonderful landscapes? I wondered. I couldn't see a way out.

It was around then that it happened.

"It's you—you're the one, the poisoning victim!"

The writer, who was middle-aged, obviously meant no harm, and I think he was just trying to make conversation. We'd never met before. I'd only paid him a visit at his home to pick up a manuscript in place of his usual editor, who was off work with appendicitis. He repeated his comment and invited me inside, and I felt myself starting to sweat.

Still, as an editor, I could hardly ask an author if we could change the subject.

Actually, the only remaining sign of the incident was that people kept asking me the same questions about it, which took quite a toll on my heavy body. If I'd been my usual healthy self, it wouldn't have fazed me at all. But in my lethargic state, even small things felt weighty and burdensome.

"That's me, but it all happened so quickly, and they took care of me at the hospital, so it hardly feels like it. Plus, since I wasn't targeted personally, it really feels like something that didn't have much to do with me. Almost like getting bitten by a dog, or being in a car accident," I said.

"So did you see the face of the guy that did it?"

He and his wife were looking at me with intense curiosity.

Their eyes looked my face up and down. Their

gazes seemed to stick to my skin. *It's only natural they're curious—if someone like me turned up at my house I'd look at them like that, too,* I thought, but I still couldn't meet their eyes. I was in a strange house being stared at by people I didn't know. It was uncomfortable.

"Yes, I did. But he seemed so different from when we worked together before, I didn't recognize him. I wouldn't have dreamed he'd come back to the staff cafeteria to do that."

Even though it was me saying all of this, my voice sounded distant, like someone else just saying words that the people in front of me might like to hear.

They had more questions.

"So you weren't the editor who took over working with that young woman writer?"

"I wonder what the company would have had to do if more people had eaten the curry and suffered the same effects."

"What was he like when he worked there? Did he show any signs of cracking up?"

"How did it feel to swallow that much flu medicine? How lethal is that stuff, really, anyway?"

"Do you believe he never intended to kill? Do

you think he would have acquired a more deadly poison, if he had?"

At first I'd made an effort to come up with appropriate-sounding answers, but my mind started to go blank and I was having trouble speaking. I wanted to speak, but I couldn't get any words out of my mouth. I was besieged by an indescribable annoyance. I was so frustrated by the whole situation that I just wanted to walk out of my own body. Just like that night with Yu in the hospital room, when my anger had turned explosive, everything seemed to get out of control.

I took the cup of tea I'd been drinking and threw it hard against the floor.

The pretty cup shattered at great speed, and the sound of it hurt me, more than anyone else, more than I could express.

The cup was broken, and I was devastated.

It had been so pretty, and now it was irreparably broken. I couldn't turn back time or quell the waves of emotion that had been stirred up in me.

I started to fidget violently, and the author hurriedly came and held me to stop me moving. But I kept squirming in his arms and started to cry loudly.

"I'm tired of questions. I'm sick of them!"

I was nearly shouting.

But the other me was calm. I was watching things unfold from a short distance away, in a slight cold sweat.

This was the author's home. I was a lowly editor who was here to pick up his manuscript. And here I was, breaking a visitor's teacup and crying, and shouting, and causing a scene.

This made me no different from Mr. Yamazoe . . . They'd have to fire me. But it wasn't as though I could do anything to stop myself just now. I felt helpless.

I rushed out of the author's arms, fell to the floor, and pummeled it with my hands, still crying.

I didn't care anymore.

But then something unexpected happened.

The writer's wife crouched down and knelt beside me on the floor. Then she cradled my head and stroked it. Over and over, with utter kindness, like you would do to a small child. And she said, "I'm so sorry. It was insensitive of us."

There were tears in her eyes. She turned to the writer with a stern expression and said, "You were in the wrong there. All those questions to someone who'd been through something like that."

"I apologize. It was out of an excess of curiosity," he said, looking genuinely apologetic and regretful. "I freely admit it was beneath me. I'm sorry."

Still crying, trying to catch my breath through the tears, I said, *Your cup, I broke it. I'll pay for it, and of course you can tell the company, I'm so sorry. I'm not quite back to normal yet, I think I must have been tired. I know it doesn't excuse my behavior. Please ask them to deal with me as I deserve.*

I managed to get these words out somehow. The two of them shook their heads and said, *No, we're the ones that should be apologizing. We're old enough to be your parents; we should have known better than to pester you with questions without even considering how you must feel about it . . .* They sat on the floor with me and kept reassuring me, looking serious.

"You know, it just occurred to me that we live in an age when someone you meet and speak to in the normal course of things might be struck down at any minute, and then that set me thinking, and I couldn't help but wonder, and since we'd never met before I suppose I felt a little disinhibited, which was very insensitive of me. I admit I can't help but indulge my curiosity sometimes. It's a hazard of being a writer. I can only apologize," he said. "It was quite inexcusable of me, when you've been through so much. Let's forget about the whole thing, sit down, and have some more tea."

"Don't worry about the cup," his wife said. "It's nothing compared with what happened to you." She discreetly cleared away its remains and brought out hot coffee with milk from the kitchen. Then she served some rich candied chestnuts in a beautiful dish. "Let's all have these and make up."

I was too embarrassed to even look at her, but once I'd chewed and swallowed a few chestnuts, I felt warmer and more comfortable.

The worst thing for me was that I'd been unaware of how badly I was doing. On top of that, I'd made a display of myself in front of people I'd never met.

I understood for the first time then that when you'd narrowly escaped death, met with the police, been reminded of things from the past you'd rather not remember, appeared on the news, and been asked all kinds of invasive questions, you couldn't simply keep on living life as though nothing had happened.

I should really have said yes to that counseling, I thought, feeling chagrined.

The deeper I sank into my shame, the kinder the author and his wife seemed to become.

"There's nothing at all for you to apologize for, it's totally understandable. We were utterly insensitive. I wouldn't have blamed you if you'd taken it out on one of us. I am so sorry."

The author's wife continued comforting me, and the author nodded emphatically at everything she said.

Shrinking as small as I possibly could, I bowed to them and made my excuses.

Of course, I didn't dare tell Yu about it, and I went to bed still so mortified that I tossed and turned all night. I wished I could have erased the day altogether.

At the same time . . .

If I put aside what I'd done, I could clearly recall their earnest faces—innocent, like children who'd made up after a fight—and the wife's gentle touch as she stroked my head. It made me feel suddenly tender, as though someone had handed me a bunch of flowers when I wasn't expecting anything.

I'd thought of them as smug, insensitive people

who took people's stories and turned them into bestsellers. But when I'd inadvertently exposed my vulnerability to them, they'd done the same, and we'd met one another like children, equal in age and position.

I finally had an inkling of why his books were so popular.

Maybe—in all the time that they looked like they were conforming to the rules of society—people were really exchanging something much more precious with one another that lay behind what appeared on the surface.

I knew full well that what I'd done was beyond the pale.

But I could sense how, that day—just when I'd been in danger of slipping onto a strange and hopeless path like Mr. Yamazoe had done—a morsel of human goodness, working within this world where there were no reasons and no guarantees, had lifted me up and saved me.

"You look like you're still struggling."

One afternoon, sometime after the teacup incident, a manager named Mr. Sasamoto suddenly spoke to me in the hallway at work. Mr. Sasamoto had had a stroke last year, but had returned fully to work, with only the slightest trouble getting his mouth around words sometimes.

"It seems my liver's still struggling, but I'm feeling much better," I said. "It's good to see you looking well."

"Thank you. Can we talk?" Mr. Sasamoto asked.

"Of course, I'm free now."

"Let's go to the lounge," he said.

I had a bad feeling about this.

Mr. Sasamoto was the manager closest to Shibayama, the editor assigned to that author and who'd been in the hospital with appendicitis that day.

The lounge was nearly empty, with just one pair of people having a meeting.

Mr. Sasamoto sat on the deep sofa and took a sip of his green tea. Then he said, "This hasn't come through Shibayama. The author's wife got in touch directly—she told me what happened. Is everything all right?"

"Yes, I'm more than prepared on that count," I said.

"His wife and mine are friends, and she often comes to visit, you see. Of course, she's smart, and hasn't said anything to my wife, nor does she think it's something you need to be punished for. She was very concerned about you, and even apologized to me. So I thought I'd check in. You haven't been pushing yourself too hard?"

"I'm doing my best," I said, "but I have to admit I'm not fully recovered yet, and my confidence has been suffering."

Mr. Sasamoto nodded.

"He can be tactless sometimes because he has a quick mind and found success early in his career. I expect he let his curiosity get the better of him, like a child, and didn't mean to cause harm with his questions," Mr. Sasamoto said.

"I know that," I said. "I think it's one of the wonderful things about him, and I really should have been able to respond in the way it was intended. I've caused a lot of trouble."

Following the incident, I'd sent the author and his wife a set of good teacups—a set that wouldn't have come close to costing what the one I broke was worth, but which would do for everyday use. I knew that didn't cancel out what I'd done, so I was somewhat prepared. I imagined I'd need to visit them again to apologize formally, along with Mr. Sasamoto. But what he said was this:

"If you still find you're tired, or struggling mentally, I'll ask the president to give you some time off. Needless to say, I haven't mentioned this to him, nor do I plan to. I've said so to the author, and they're not upset, either. In fact, they're most apologetic, so you've got nothing to worry about. I'll make sure you can always take a break and then come back, so don't overthink it, just come talk to me."

"That's very kind of you."

He wants me to go before I cause any more problems, I thought. It was all too obvious what he was really saying. I was reeling. I would almost have preferred to have gotten chewed out and fired.

Gently, Mr. Sasamoto persisted.

"You're a victim here. You probably don't want to think of it that way, and would prefer to put it behind you, but it did happen, so you mustn't overdo it. I worked with Yamazoe for a long time, but I was too busy with my own recovery to help him. On some level, I'm responsible, or involved, too. I don't mean to treat you like another Yamazoe, but I wanted to help in any way I can."

"Thank you. I'll give it some thought."

"I mean, I've been on the receiving end of the author's bombardments myself, and they're quite something. When I had my stroke, he wanted to know everything about it," Mr. Sasamoto said, laughing.

"But I wasn't in my right mind that day," I said. "I'll think hard about it. It might be better for the company if I take some time off."

"Good, good. It's just an idea. If you're managing, that's fine too. But the matter of the other day, that's all closed, just so you know. There was another thing I wanted to tell you," he said, his face brightening at the change of topic. "I go to a Chinese medicine clinic where they prescribe all kinds of herbal remedies. I think they really help. I can introduce you, if you'd like. I think that tradition would know about detoxifying the body in a way that doesn't burden the liver, so if you're still feeling fatigued, it might be worth a visit."

Mr. Sasamoto had been a good person even before his stroke, but he'd been quite tetchy and could get curt or speak too fast when things got busy, making people want to stay out of his way. When he came back from being in the hospital, he'd changed a little. He showed his emotions more on his face, and his color was better, and maybe because he couldn't speak as quickly as he'd used to, he'd started to slow down and get things done more calmly.

Previously some people would imitate his fast talking and make fun of him, but these days he blended in more, and his reputation was that he'd become a lot easier to work with since his illness. Of course, that was a pretty impersonal way of looking at it, but the new Mr. Sasamoto would probably have taken even that in stride. He seemed to be living now within some far bigger picture.

So there I was, feeling a little rejected from thinking I'd been told to stay away from work, but also feeling kind of moved by it, too.

I'd been so preoccupied by what was going on inside myself, but at work, amid the difficult people, there were also people like Mr. Sasamoto, who noticed when others were going through things, and tried to help.

This man, who'd been so demanding and easy to annoy, had nearly died, then recovered, and was here, with kindly eyes, smiling at me. And I was lucky to be alive to be touched by his kindness.

The whole thing seemed like some kind of wonderful miracle.

"That's kind of you. But are you sure? I don't want to cause you any trouble," I said.

"I won't make a formal introduction or anything

like that, of course, but I'll give you their card. Go see them when you're ready. Even knowing you can go there in a pinch takes some of the pressure off, doesn't it?" Mr. Sasamoto said, and handed me the clinic's business card.

The card was warm from being in his pocket.

Only a year ago, he must have had to do a lot of thinking about life and death. About his wife and kids, their home, or the work he was going to do— all of these things.

I felt that I was being handed the perspective that had been borne of his experience.

"Thank you," I said.

He raised one hand in the air as he walked away.

I was amazed to think, now, that I'd been going through life believing I understood anything about people, only to have nearly been killed by one of them, and then saved by several others. The whole chain of events seemed like the plot of some made-up story.

Good days followed bad days.

Old lovers called after seeing me on the news, but only out of curiosity rather than concern, and I would feel blue; then a girl who lived next door when we were children sent me a message to say she was surprised to see me on TV, but that she was glad I was alive and looking well.

I felt like I was no longer at risk of causing a scene.

The heaviness was still with me, but I went to the clinic that Mr. Sasamoto recommended, and took the detoxifying prescription they gave me, and my color started to improve. And things around me started to quiet down.

That whole time, I'd find myself looking up at the sky and thinking.

What if it had been arsenic or cyanide in the curry instead of flu medicine, and I'd had to leave this world behind, having been taken totally unawares?

The sky was blue and clear and shining, with clouds streaked across it like they'd been drawn on with a flat brush, and contrails corkscrewed against the blue like lamb's tails, and the wind blew through high above the ground.

At times like these, I could forget the heaviness I'd become habituated to, and be in the world with every part of my body.

But really, nothing would have changed. The world would have continued the way it always had been. Mr. Yamazoe's crime would have been heavier. Grandma and Grandpa might have cried all day and aged before their time. They'd remember me and wonder why I'd been taken before them, and put a curse on Mr. Yamazoe's life. Grandma would work herself to the bone for days on end, painstakingly going through my belongings, crying all the while. She would fold each of my clothes and send them to get dry-cleaned. She would polish my jewelry, pack my crockery into boxes, and, with her smooth hands, and the attention to detail that I loved, would bring order to the mess of things I'd left behind. As though she were soothing me.

And Yu would be left alone in our apartment.

He'd eat dinner alone and wash the dishes that we used to eat from together, alone. He'd fall asleep alone in our bed, and on his days off he'd go alone to the swimming pool where we used to go together and stop by the bookstore on the way home like we always did.

Picturing it was bringing tears to my eyes.

Someday he'd get together with someone younger and far more beautiful than me and tell her the tragic story of how, years ago, a woman he was

about to marry had been poisoned and died—a secret that he'd strengthen their bond by revealing.

But me—I'd disappear from Yu's life. Yu going
home to our apartment after my funeral. Yu with
shoulders hunched, looking lonely in black mourn-
ing clothes. Yu keeping our apartment clean the way
he always did, but only for himself. Yu, who'd never
be able to eat my pasta again.

I'd always believed I didn't take up a lot of space
in this world—that it hardly mattered whether
I was here or not. When a person left, the people
around them got used to their absence. That was
true enough.

But when I pictured the world without me, and
the people I loved living on in it, I couldn't help but
feel like crying.

The only thing missing from these tableaux was
me, but suddenly they looked much lonelier. And
even if the hole I left was only temporary, until the
other characters all moved on into the unknown future, the space where I belonged suddenly seemed
to harbor a rare glow.

It felt as precious as trees, or sunlight, or cats I
met on the street.

Astonished by this revelation, I looked up at the

sky again and again. Here I was, with a body, looking up at the sky. I existed.

As beautiful as the sun setting in the distance,
life lived inside this, the only body I would ever
have.

Yu was on a business trip for a couple of weeks, and
I was home alone for the first time in a while.

I'd lived with my grandma and grandpa for a
long time, and then when I'd saved up enough to
get my own apartment, I met Yu fairly soon after
that, so I'd never actually lived alone for very long. It
was a nice change. I brought home more work than
usual, and worked, ate, and did laundry when I felt
like it. I felt less lonely than I'd expected.

But at odd moments, alone in the big apartment
we rented together, I found myself thinking, *What
am I doing here?*

When I mentioned that Yu was away on a business trip, Grandma and Grandpa got on my case to
visit, so the first weekend I went home to see them.

Home, to me, meant their place, the home I grew
up in.

I helped Grandpa weed his garden and ate a lot

of sticky rice that Grandma made. Grandma and I went to the local bathhouse and scrubbed each other's backs. The skin on hers was smooth, and the water rolled cleanly off it when I rinsed the soap away. It seemed youthful, and made me feel like she was going to be around for a good long while, which was a relief.

Then, all warm, we watched the sunset as we slowly walked home together through the town where I'd grown up, doing our shopping along the way.

"I'm in the mood for strawberries," I said, and Grandma happily bought us two containers of them.

And when we had sukiyaki for dinner, we finished it up by adding rice at the end, and mixing it into the broth, like we always did. We told one another how it looked a mess and tasted beautiful. We mashed the boiled potatoes into it, too, and ate until we were full.

Then we talked a little about the incident, and the two of them quizzed me about whether the company really was a safe place to work, and whether I should look for another job.

It was fine, I told them, since if that kind of thing were a regular occurrence, the company would have gone under a long time ago, so I wanted to stay there. Of course, I didn't tell them about having an outburst and causing a scene at an important author's home.

Then we talked about Yu, and they had a lot of questions about whether we were going to have a wedding, when we were going to get married, and if we wanted to have children.

We haven't made plans like that, I said, but we're thinking of just having a dinner for family, and registering the marriage at the registry office, to save having a big party with people from work, and everything. I told them how I'd gotten to know his mom, and that she and her second husband seemed to be a good couple. Yu and I were thinking about having a meal at a hotel with them and my grandma and grandpa.

"How wonderful," Grandma said. "I've been waiting for this!"

But none of us brought up my real mother. Both Grandma and Grandpa were committed to pretending she didn't exist.

They were my dad's parents, and he'd died when I was very young.

•

"Mama!"

I slept in my own bed in my room at home for the first time in a long time.

My faded poster of John Lennon from when I'd been a fan was still up on the wall. The desk my grandparents had gotten me when I was in middle school was still there like it always had been, and it made me feel nostalgic and almost nervous.

I'd changed into an old pair of pajamas, which Grandma had washed and folded for me, and my belly was full, and for the first time in a while, I'd forgotten how heavy my body felt.

Maybe I will take that vacation time I've got saved up, and have a break, like Mr. Sasamoto said, I thought. Even if I left enough for our honeymoon, which should be happening soon, I could probably be away for about a month.

Ironically, starting to feel a little better had made me realize how sick I'd been, and how I'd been ignoring that to keep going to work.

If I go to Mr. Sasamoto and tell him I'm ready to stop being stubborn, I thought, it might be doable, maybe even okay, since we weren't even that busy just now.

Then I could spend some time going to bed and getting up whenever I wanted, maybe make pasta from scratch like Yu loved to eat, and take it easy for a while. It wasn't every day a person had to go through an ordeal like mine, so maybe I deserved it. Maybe it had even confused the people around me that I hadn't done it already.

And the scene I'd caused—when I was convinced I was fine!—was more than enough reason in itself to take a break. I was lucky things hadn't turned out worse, because if I'd done that in front of the wrong person I really would have gotten fired. This was probably exactly the right time to play it safe, just in case.

Being back at home for the first time in a while, my heart seemed to be unwinding. I even wondered, *Why didn't I think of this before?*

It reminded me of something I'd read in a book, about how children that have been abused learned to detach their minds from physical pain.

It occurred to me that maybe that was why I didn't notice how fatigued I was, or why I felt guilty about being lazy when it wasn't even my fault but because my liver was still recovering. I felt my mind go quiet.

•

My dad died suddenly of a heart attack when I was four. He was a director of the company that Grandpa ran, and they'd been really busy at work.

My birth mother was twenty years younger than him, and grew up sheltered, without even having really done much housework, or ever lived away from her parents. They agreed to her getting married because she got pregnant with me, but from what I heard, she had trouble adjusting to motherhood. She always looked as though she were holding someone else's baby, they said.

But of course, that came from Grandma and Grandpa, who were hardly neutral parties.

Grandma and Grandpa had never had any confidence in my dad's hasty match with my obviously immature mother. They'd been against the marriage from the start, and had always been ready to take me in if the need arose.

What's strange is that I don't have any sad memories from that time.

I remember my mother crying after my dad died, and me crying with her. I remember her taking me gently into her arms, putting her cheek on mine, and sleeping next to me and holding my hand.

I know she had pale skin, a high voice, and a soft figure with large hips.

I remember her singing lullabies, and us dancing and singing along together to children's programs on TV.

So—for whatever reason—I have no negative associations about my time with her.

But I'm told it wasn't actually like that.

I can't figure out at this point what the truth was. I don't even know how much really happened, and how much I made up.

There are things I know only as facts. At kindergarten, I was monitored extra carefully because I always had bruises and burns on my body.

When my injuries escalated to broken bones, the authorities took my mother into custody straight from the hospital where she was crying at my bedside.

Then, once I left the hospital, I was immediately taken in by Grandma and Grandpa.

I suppose what my mother ought to have done when my dad died was to take me and go back to her parents. But her younger sister, with whom she didn't get along very well, had just gotten married and moved back in. So she decided to try and prove she could make it on her own, only to struggle with raising me to the point that she became quite seriously unstable.

I understand there were trials and hospitalizations and things, but my mother disappeared from my life forever. I imagine she's alive somewhere—with her parents, or remarried—but Grandma and Grandpa, who were absolutely furious at the time, never forgave her. The only way they could come to terms with what happened seemed to be to cut all ties, and treat her as someone who had never existed.

It left me with no choice but to follow their lead if I wanted to be worthy of their unreserved devotion.

Even so, I still remember the feeling of the lovely house where I lived with my real parents. The white walls, vases kept full of flowers, a big leather sofa, and blue drapes.

I often thought, *If only I could remember her hurting me.* Then, at least, I would be able to think badly of her; hate her, even.

I can recall the pain of the broken bones. I had gotten overexcited about something, vomited—and then came the pain. After that the only images I have are of my mother crying and begging for forgiveness, the sour smell of her sweat, a feeling of being held very tightly in someone's arms, the sound of the ambulance, and being asked so many questions by different adults.

Given that this is all I have, I hardly think I could be expected to blame her.

I was finally drifting off when my phone rang.

I picked up and heard Yu's voice.

"Were you asleep?"

"Yeah, old folks go to bed early, so I went to bed, too."

"Sorry, sorry, I've just gotten back to the hotel. How is it there?"

"It's like being a kid again. They keep feeding me things I like. I think I might have gained weight," I said. "Yu, are you okay to talk right now?"

"Sure I am. Except I'm in my underpants, so I'll be getting dressed while we talk."

"Yeah, keep warm. So it seems like I'm not really back to full speed, health-wise," I said. I decided not to mention what had happened at the writer's home, because that was about work. "My boss said I could take some vacation time. I'm thinking about doing it."

"That sounds like a good idea. If you can, I think you should. To tell you the truth, I was worried you were pushing yourself too hard, going straight back to work after it happened. If you want to have a career, part of your job is to rest when you can."

"Maybe I should have done it sooner, but I'm at a place where I feel like I can do it now."

"Of course. You've seemed so tired this whole time. And when you feel like that you don't even have the energy to think straight, do you? But in that case," he said, "not that we should just because it's convenient, but what do you think about using the time to get married and have our honeymoon? I know it would move things up slightly."

"Really? But we decided to try living together for a year before we get married! You agreed," I said.

Then I caught myself. I noticed how adamantly I resisted changing my mind about something I'd already decided on. And how that stubbornness stopped me from being able to listen to the people around me.

A pleasant wave called flexibility washed over my heart.

At nearly the same time, Yu said, "You could have died!" He sounded exasperated. "You've been through something huge. Do we really need to be sticking to plans we made before it all? Why do you need to be so rigid about it?"

"You've got a point," I said, humbly.

"You never take yourself into account," he said. "If you're asking for vacation time, you should tell them that given what happened, you need a break, and you're going to get married while you're at it. We can go to Hawai'i or somewhere."

"I'd be happy with the hot springs in Atami."

"Let's think about that later. I can take a couple of weeks off anytime, or if we're not having a ceremony we can do a reception on the weekend. I mean, we can work out the details when I'm back."

I heard the rustling sounds of Yu getting changed.

I could picture him, alone in the room, half naked, talking about wedding plans.

"That's great. Thanks. Good night."

"Good night."

The reason I was too cautious, and rigid, and couldn't see myself clearly, and was terrified of being happy—maybe it was all because I didn't remember.

But I didn't know a lot of people who had memories from when they were three or four.

Of course it was sad to be estranged from my real mother, but there was a good reason, after all, and since she never tried to get in touch, either, she was obviously living a new life. As long as she was happy, that was probably fine.

I knew Grandma and Grandpa would never want to talk to her, even if I was getting married. She simply was no longer part of my life.

Those were the thoughts I'd lived by up till now—that bygones were bygones. I told myself things were good as they were, like I always did.

I always liked to think that I was allowed to have a happy, peaceful life after what I'd been through as a child—that life owed me that much, even.

But once I got a serious boyfriend, the kind who would call me from a business trip and try to get me to see that I mattered, I started to doubt whether I really deserved to be thought of in that way. I didn't question why, for instance, I always went to bed when he did, no matter how busy I was.

I sometimes wondered whether this had something to do with my mother.

There was nothing I could do about it.

Maybe that was why I sometimes felt like I couldn't breathe, and like I needed to get out. It seemed like even I didn't know what to do with myself a lot of the time.

What would I do if I had another unexpected outburst? Or if I gave in to a self-destructive impulse, like Mr. Yamazoe had? If I had a child, would I lose control and hurt them? What if I said something terribly hurtful to Yu?

I drifted into thoughts about my vacation time and getting married, and life in general, and by the time I thought I should get up and turn the lights off before I fell asleep, I'd forgotten all about thoughts of my birth mother. I got up and switched off the lights.

My old room was disused and dusty, and making my throat hurt a little, so I opened the window. The fresh air came in and ran around the room, and in the sky I looked up at from the dark window, so many stars twinkled. *Hey, it's beautiful*, I thought. The clear air filled my lungs, making my entire body feel cool, and somehow cleansed.

It must have been the stale air that filled me with doubts.

Whatever it was that still lingered in my liver must

have come from the poison that had secretly lain dormant inside me all these years, and the poison that had been within Mr. Yamazoe, my former coworker. Unlucky coincidences like this one happened all the time. He and I had become entangled out of some tiny accident of fate, and the toxin had circulated through my body ever since, sapping me of my energy.

On the other hand, I was fortunate to have been surrounded by enough small happinesses to keep me fulfilled, in spite of the circumstances.

These dark thoughts would disappear once I got some rest and let my body recover. The blood running through my body would be clean, like the night air, and I'd be stronger than I was before. I'd get rid of all the old poison while I was at it. Now was as good a time as any.

Satisfied, I closed the window and burrowed down under the warm covers, and went to sleep.

I went to sleep and had a strange dream.

I was in the living room in the house I hardly remembered—the house I lived in when I was really young.

In the dream, I was at a white table with my real

parents, eating dinner. In the background the evening news was chattering on TV.

I couldn't really see my dad's face, but he'd changed out of his suit into casual clothes and looked relaxed. I felt him there, a solid, loving presence.

I was in my own little chair, eating rice from a bowl with my own spoon. The bowl was small and decorated with pictures of elephants.

My parents were chatting amicably about something. I was watching them or watching TV, eating in silence.

The rice had some darker grains mixed in. The stuff called black rice. In the dream my mother was the kind of person who was interested in health, and often cooked our rice with other grains mixed in.

She and I spotted it at almost the same time.

The black rice in my bowl had legs.

"What's that? What's in your food? I only cooked white rice today!" my mother said, alarmed. "Those are insects! Don't eat them! Stop, spit them out!"

My mother held out her hand, and I shuddered and quickly spat out the mouthful of rice into her palm. Then I flung the bowl away from me and jumped into her lap.

"Mama! Mama, Mama!" I put my arms around her neck and clung to her tightly.

She seemed not to mind at all that I'd spat out the mouthful of rice full of insects into her hand, and simply turned it out into a napkin and hugged me.

"I'm sorry, I didn't notice there were bugs in the rice," she said gently. "I'm so sorry. That was scary. It was my fault."

My father looked at us, smiling. "Little girl, you really ate those bugs, huh?" he said. "Sorry, but that's the funniest thing I've heard all week!"

"You might have eaten some yourself."

"As long as they were cooked through, what's the harm?" He shrugged.

"Really!"

"I know housework isn't your forte, but you could at least make sure the rice is fresh. You must have used an old bag."

"I'm so sorry, I can't imagine how it happened. There, there. Don't worry, it'll never happen again. This doesn't mean I don't care about you, far from it. It just means I'm not very good at cooking rice, and I made a mistake. My precious little one, I love you. Please forgive me," she said.

Then I smiled through my tears, and although my throat felt scratchy, my mother's lap and neck were warm, and I stayed there, letting her hold me tight.

When I woke up, for a second, I could still vividly feel the sensation of my arms around my mother's neck, and my chest against hers. I was overcome by such a deep yearning that I cried as much as I'd ever cried in my life. In my old room at Grandma and Grandpa's, with just a wall separating me from where they were sleeping, I wailed.

I cried harder than I ever did when I got my heart broken, or when I broke down at the writer's home.

Of course, I knew that the dream was just a dream, a mixture of different things that were going on for me right now, and that it never happened that way.

But I cried and cried.

Was I feeling sorry for myself, for having been abused and abandoned by my mother? Or was I moved by how I'd managed to live my life until now in spite of all that?

Of course that was part of it.

But the dream was the kind of dream that made everything else disappear. It was so soft, so sweet, and so true that it wiped out all the bad memories I must have had of my dim and unclear childhood. In the dream, the three of us were utterly warm and gentle with one another, and happiness filled the space between us like a globe of light.

My dad never meant to die and leave us, and my mother didn't really want to hurt me, and if I'd had my way we'd all have lived together as a family for as long as we wanted.

All prospects of our impossible castle of love were squeezed into that little dream.

It contained all my true feelings inside it, like a ripe fruit ready for harvesting.

Everything was safe. The three of them would live inside that dream forever.

It was just as real my life outside, in the present day.

Through the mess of my tears and sobs, I knew this to be true. I was sure of it.

The hot tears streaming down my face washed away the poison inside me. I finally felt ready to start a life of my own.

Whether or not the feeling was real, or just an illusion, I believed in it.

•

Pretty soon, my grandma would get up, and the smell of miso soup would rise from the kitchen. Grandpa would start his morning calisthenics. But until then, I'd return to sleep and let the morning light wake me. I felt as though all the toxicity that had been stored in my body for years, which had been brought to the surface by the poison in the curry, had been cleared out along with my tears. I closed my swollen eyelids and drowsily went back to sleep.

Since then, things have been good.

In the long term, of course, there are no guarantees. Every life has its share of problems, and there's no way of knowing when that same distress might pass through me again. It's possible another illness might trigger another upset. For the time being, though, these fears were dormant, and the days passed peacefully.

I took my vacation time a month later, went out for a peaceful meal with the family I had now, and went to the city office with Yu the next morning to register our marriage.

Then we went to Hawai'i for our honeymoon, and when we came back, I was tanned and healthy-looking and five pounds heavier. I met up with Mitsuko for lunch in the cafeteria and gave her the souvenirs I'd gotten for her.

I was back at full capacity at work as well, and while my coworkers joked that getting poisoned had turned out to be a blessing in disguise, now that I was married, I'm enjoying keeping busy every day.

I often wonder why it had to happen to me.

Looking back, I felt like everything that day seems to have happened in an instant, so there would have been no stopping it.

Things followed from one another as if by magic. That was why, even now that it was over, it was like I'd had a strange dream, and it was still hard to tell whether it had been hard or not.

Of course, I had regrets.

If only I'd been paying a little more attention. If only I'd chosen a different dish. If only I'd gotten there five minutes later—then none of it might have happened. My life would have carried on as usual.

Like many people after going through some calamity, I realized that I'd never appreciated how peaceful and precious my life had been before.

I learned firsthand how destructive it was to not be fully well. It was like a flu where you had a low-grade fever for weeks, where it wasn't that you couldn't get up, or work, or laugh, or cry. You just constantly felt heavy, and fuzzy in your head. So it was impossible to do anything. It had been all I could do to simply get through the days until my mind felt clearer.

Either way, I'd never been the kind of person to dwell too much on the past, and didn't have a habit of thinking too much about the future, either. So I had no idea that there was a sad and murky swamp biding its time inside me, which an unexpected trigger could bring even in a small way to the surface.

Those days—that dream—had exposed something that had been inside me and changed it.

Just like a pet bird that had accidentally ventured out of its cage, the incident had cast me out of the world that I had known.

Outside, it was dark. The wind roared, and stars blinked indifferently.

•

I still ask myself whether it served me well to have stepped outside the birdcage of my life, even just temporarily, given that I was always going to go back inside it.

But the answer is always the same.

"It was right," I hear a kind voice say.

From nowhere in particular, repeatedly, like a lullaby, as though to confirm that I'm alive. It comes through soft and swift, like how in spring the trees and plants bud and the whole world turns bright green.

So I close my eyes for a little while, and think about this world of mine that—by a strange turn of fate—I ended up seeing from the outside. And I offer up a prayer for the people who've left it over the years.

People who slipped past me, even though we might have been able to spend more time if things had been different. My real parents, old lovers, former friends. Maybe my connection with Mr. Yamazoe belonged with them, too.

The ways our paths happened to cross in this world meant that things could never have worked out between us.

But in some other world, far away, deep, deep down, by some clear waterside, I know we're together—smiling, feeling kind, and being good to one another.

Not Warm at All

I've been earning my living mostly as a writer for about five years now. For that reason, I'm always interested in seeing deeply into the heart of things.

Seeing into the heart of things is very different from seeing things through a personal, subjective lens. Your mind throws up all kinds of things—your own interpretations and opinions, feelings of aversion—but you let them go, and delve deeper.

Keep doing this, and at some point you reach the final prospect: the last vista of the thing, beyond which there's no farther to go.

When you get there, the air quiets, and everything becomes limpid. You start to feel a little uncertain. Surprisingly, though, no thoughts come to mind.

All you sense is that you're very much on your own. At the same time, something tells you that someone, from somewhere, at some point, once arrived at the same view.

It keeps you from feeling too lonely, but you have no way of telling whether that's a good thing or not. All you can do is look. And feel.

I was born in a town lying between mountains and a wide river, a daughter and an only child. No siblings.

My father had sold half of the land my grandfather left to him, and put the money into a bookstore where my mother also helped out. He loved books and was knowledgeable about them, and with the shop's reputation for stocking rare and unusual titles, it always did steady business, even though he ran it mostly for the joy of it.

We lived above the shop, on the second floor. I grew up surrounded by the presence of books, inside the dry smell and the silence that soaks up sound particular to spaces full of paper.

My health was delicate, and I didn't really enjoy playing outside with the neighborhood kids, so I spent much of my childhood quietly borrowing books from the shop and leafing through them in my room.

From my window I had a view of the river.

A river is a strange thing. It invariably harbors a quality of menace that can make your hair stand on end. Even on clear days, when the water flowed smoothly and the sunlight glinted off the shallows and made the plants on the bank sparkle, I always felt that the river was somehow connected to something dark, deep, and frightening.

And yet, when I traveled to other cities, I always found that a view without a river was of no interest to me at all.

Perhaps that was because the inherent stillness of my nature made me crave the sight of things that moved.

I lived in Paris for just a few years as an adult to study the language. I'd fallen in love with French literature and yearned to read it in the original. I also had the notion that to be interested in the literature without ever having been to Paris was faintly embarrassing, if commonplace, like an Italian restaurant where the chef had never been to Italy.

That was when I learned how easily I could slip into feeling at home in a city with a river flowing through it.

I also discovered that sitting in a café watching people go by was just like watching a river.

It could only happen in a city with a long history.

The sight of modern-day people streaming past old, weighty buildings of frightening shapes and colors—that was exactly what a river was.

It was how I came to understand that what made a river frightening was the chilling infinitude of time itself.

In a similar vein, I once spent a long time thinking about light.

I used to ponder things like this, mull over them endlessly, because I had time on my hands. I'd felt very out of place in Japan, since I hadn't known many people who did that, but in Paris, I met many people that were like me. There, I could feel that pursuing your own interests or preoccupations, instead of treating them as somehow shameful, would make life easier and lighter, so I quit being embarrassed about engaging in these seemingly useless thoughts.

When I did that, the world suddenly blossomed into pink.

The rose-colored world where I lived had space and dimension, and as much air to breathe as I wanted, and multitudes of things that opened and closed with dizzying speed.

That space constricted a little when I spent time with other people, but it wasn't a problem, because I knew I could quickly return to that world of my own.

That was how I became a writer, and finally found a place to belong.

In the picture books I read as a child, lights seen in the distance always represented the promise of warmth.

A person lost in the mountains spots a glimmer among the trees, or a solitary wanderer suddenly feels homesick at the glow and voices coming from a stranger's home.

Of course, in some stories there's a twist, and frightening things follow. But that feeling of seeing a light in the darkness is always the same. A universally understood, eternal warmth.

●

On that count, there's a memory about which I have complicated feelings to this day.

When I was young, I had just one friend. He was a boy, so you could call him my first love.

His name was Makoto. He was an incredibly quiet and gentle boy, and often sick. Makoto was the beloved son of a family that for generations had made the kind of high-class *wagashi* used in tea ceremonies. His sister, who was twelve years older, and smart and outgoing and passionate about the world of traditional confectionery, was to succeed the family business. This meant the family was all the more protective of Makoto and his tender and winsome nature, as the baby of the family—the bonus child.

Although I didn't know the details, it seemed that Makoto had actually been born to his father's mistress. Since it would have been unwise to leave a boy child outside the family, given their standing, they had paid her off and taken him in.

I can only imagine how difficult the situation would have been for his parents. But they dealt with it discreetly and didn't treat Makoto differently at all. They doted on him just as they did his siblings, and in turn he warmed the hearts of everyone around him and brought them together, almost like a beloved pet.

More than anything, I think that was down to his being easy to love.

You couldn't help but be smitten by his angelic demeanor, and his endlessly sweet disposition.

For instance, if the housekeeper swatted at a cockroach, Makoto would watch her do it with tears brimming in his eyes. Then he'd say something precocious, like *I just felt my life and that roach's life swap places.*

His mother used to tell my mother that he seemed to have been born with a Buddhist view of things. *I'll send him to a temple once he's old enough, as long as he doesn't mind*, she'd said. *The discipline will build him up, and who knows, he might even go far as a monk.*

When Makoto helped weed the garden, he'd pull up each plant with utmost attention and all its roots intact. And afterward the patch that he had weeded would look divinely clear compared with everyone else's, as though everything was at ease there, and the air moved through it with no effort at all. Like a space that had been cleansed through a collaboration of man and nature.

Our friendship consisted mostly of me going over to Makoto's house with piles of books and comics.

Once in a while, we'd walk along the river, holding hands. No arguments or roughhousing, no bursting into song. We simply walked.

I remember how Makoto's sweaty hand, small and soft, would slowly dry out as I held it in mine.

I felt like it was my duty to keep him safe.

Once, he said to me, "Mitsuyo, there's something round and beautiful and lonely inside of you. Kind of like a firefly."

I asked him, "Can you always see it?"

And he said, "No, only when we're quiet. It's nice to look at."

I was slightly disappointed that it wasn't my face or anything he liked to look at, but even so, his words made me about as happy as if he'd said he was in love with me.

After that, there were many times when I would

catch Makoto gazing at me dreamily, with his big clear eyes and his surprisingly thick brows drawn into a neat line, and I would know that he was looking at the glow of my soul, or whatever it was.

Then all of a sudden, I would feel free from all the anxieties that weighed on my mind—about being kidnapped, or the homework I hadn't done, or my parents fighting and maybe getting divorced—as though I was being shielded from them.

By a strong, bright, rose-colored light.

It was only much later that I learned the light came from me, and what Makoto had done was to be its witness and protector.

Every time I walked past Makoto's enormous house, I would look for the lights on in each of its windows, and something in me would breathe a sigh of relief.

That house belongs to a family that has been there for generations, I'd think to myself. *There's something there that stays the same even while the people come and go.*

The business employed a whole team of artisans, and every time there was an important tea ceremony or state occasion even more people would be involved in rushed preparations, and though his father might do things like stray from his marriage and bring Makoto into the world, there was a larger power there that contained all of that, swallowed it whole. No matter what happened, inside that light I saw through the windows there was, and would always be: parents, grandparents, children.

That was the feeling it gave me.

My family was just me and my parents. Mom and Dad had both moved here from outside the region, and we had no extended family nearby. So when I saw the way a large family functioned like a living system—where if one part pushed out, another would naturally respond by drawing in to accommodate it—it seemed like the embodiment of security.

Some evenings, when my family was at the table eating dinner after closing the shop, I'd be struck by how few we were. What if Dad got cancer? Or Mom worked herself into a breakdown? Then this happiness—our conversations, interspersed with sounds of the television, the clink of crockery, and moments of silence—would vanish. It felt like something that could happen all too easily, in a fell swoop.

When Makoto's great-grandfather died, he had all his other relatives around him. And when his parents were busy and away from home, there was a housekeeper to switch the lights on and put meals on the table.

But my family was just the three of us. It seemed to me like we had no backup at all.

From Makoto's point of view, things were different.

Whenever he called to say, *Let me come over to yours today*, I'd always ask, *Why? Your house is bigger, and we get much better snacks*.

He would say, *I don't know, there's just something comfortable about it*.

Child that I was, I wondered what was so comfortable about spending the afternoon reading books in my cramped and messy room, or eating my mother's homely and dry baking.

I was too naive then to pick up on the complexities of Makoto's home life.

His family didn't fit into the typical pattern of wealthy families that were cold, stiff, and transactional. I think I would have been astute enough to recognize it had that been the case. But on the contrary, their home was full of an abundance of affection that only a large, loving family could provide.

At the same time, the family business, with its various considerations, no doubt cast its subtle shadow over them all.

My family was uncomplicated, and we made our living simply. When I think back and put myself in Makoto's shoes, I imagine how safe that must have felt to him, and the feeling often brings tears to my eyes.

Some clear evenings, around the time that Venus glints like a beacon against the sky, I look at the lights in the windows of the neighborhood and remember what he used to say, and find myself wanting to cry.

You know how every single time, when it starts to get dark and it's time to go, we leave your room and go downstairs, and your dad's always there in the bookstore with some customers, and everything smells of books? And then in the kitchen window you can see the yellow glow of the light bulb, and hear your mom making dinner. That's what I always like to look at when I'm going home.

On the night I saw him for the last time, Makoto didn't want to leave.

He was so reluctant that my mother telephoned his house and offered to keep him overnight. It was quite out of character for Makoto, who was usually very good about going home when he was supposed to.

Makoto's family were always cordial to us. My father's position as an authority on old books and occasional university lecturer must have meant we were acceptable according to whatever unspoken rules they had about who they could associate with.

But it turned out that a big family gathering was to take place early the next morning, and they were keen for Makoto to come home and get a good night's sleep. And so it was arranged that the housekeeper would come to collect him.

How can I possibly describe everything that happened in the half hour before the housekeeper arrived?

Makoto had buried his face in my arm. He nestled there, with a book still open on his lap, and didn't move. He wasn't crying, just lying alongside me the way a dog does. His quiet, damp breath was making my blouse warm.

"I don't want to go, I'm scared," he said.

I stroked his fine hair carefully and told him over

and over that it was going to be okay, but I could clearly sense the air weighing heavily on us. It was as though there was some menacing presence peering in through the window. I started to feel that the two of us had been cut off from everything good—things like the lights of the world, the transparentness of dragonfly wings, perfect seasons expressed in wagashi, the luminous pale pink of cherry blossoms along the river, the way you look forward to going on vacation, the delightful feeling of knowing you're about to eat something good—and that dawn would never come.

"Let's get married someday, and then we'll never have to leave."

I knew already that marriage was something binding, and that was the very reason my parents were struggling to make theirs work, and why Makoto's parents hadn't gotten divorced after his father's affair. So I meant these words as some kind of anchor, an attempt to keep Makoto tethered to what was good in this world.

He smiled a little, shyly, and said, "I bet that would be fun. We'll spend all our time together reading and eating snacks, just like Noby and Doraemon."

"But they're both boys," I said, a little peeved at his seeming to miss the point of my romantic gesture, such as it was.

Makoto, undeterred, said dreamily, "But that's my ideal situation. They're in front of the sliding doors, lying on cushions, eating *dorayaki* and reading manga together."

"You wouldn't rather have something nicer to eat?"

"Nope, no fancy chestnuts or anything inside, and the skin's kind of soft, too. Just a regular old dorayaki," Makoto said.

Then, just for a moment, as if at a happy vision, he broke into a smile.

It unfurled like the bud of a cherry blossom: sweetly, weightlessly.

But soon the housekeeper arrived, and I watched as Makoto, dejected and on the verge of tears, walked away down the dark street, without turning to look back at me even once.

His feet dragged, and his shoulders slumped. He looked utterly forsaken.

And that was the last sight I ever had of him.

•

At night, from my window upstairs, I could catch a glimpse of Makoto's family's mansion behind the trees in their garden.

It used to reassure me to see the lights on in the house as I fell asleep. There they were, along with their long-established way of life, their meals, and the beds they slept on every night, and so they would continue to be. I felt the vision of safety including me within its protection.

But that night, for some reason, even though the lights lit up his house as usual, they brought me no peace. Just as Makoto had looked that evening, there was something bleak and lonely about their brightness reflecting vacantly off the trees.

I wonder why that is, I thought, and fell asleep. But I woke up many times during the night, each time into a sense that morning would never come. The sound of an ambulance echoed distantly against the sky.

In the morning, the neighborhood was in an uproar.

Makoto's biological mother had turned up unexpectedly, caused a huge scene trying to kidnap him, stabbed his father in the stomach, carried Makoto off in her car, and driven off a cliff edge. She had pulled off a murder-suicide, and Makoto had died with her.

His father, on the other hand, survived.

What surprised me was how life carried on the same for Makoto's family without him, almost like when his great-grandfather had died.

The shocking incident was national news. Photos of Makoto's angelic face helped the sense of tragedy, and for a while the family was the most talked-about in the country, his father portrayed in the media as the nation's most despicable dad.

So things were hectic for a while, but then they all settled back down, and the wagashi continued to sell, and the family's way of life went on as it always had.

Of course, the cloud of what happened cast its shadow on each of them.

For a long time afterward, Makoto's father could only walk hunched over and slowly, like an old man. The others would burst into tears whenever they saw me. Even the housekeeper would cry. His mother used to ask to hold me, *Just for a minute*, and take me into her arms, while his sister and brother became a lot more withdrawn.

In spite of all that, the family's prestigious wagashi store carried on without a blemish on its reputation.

This was what it took, I realized, to be something that survived.

Not just constancy, or strength.

But—like the ever-flowing river—to engulf everything that came your way and move swiftly on as though it had never been.

I'm an adult now and have an office to do my writing in, near the home where I grew up. I don't quite make a living from it, so I run workshops, and sometimes teach evening classes on French literature. A friend I was in Paris with recently opened a café nearby, and I sometimes help organize concerts there with musician friends I also met while studying abroad.

But I've still never made a friend as good as Makoto, and while I sometimes date, I've never felt as strongly for a man as I did when I told him we should get married.

I often wonder whether those that are too pure

are destined to live fleeting lives, like cats that are beautiful and white as snow, or birds with gossamer feathers.

For all the nobleness of his spirit, Makoto was just a boy. He was just a boy when he cried that he was afraid to go home, and just a boy when he died. I've carried this fact around in my chest ever since.

If I ever come to love someone enough to want to marry, I'd like to name our child after my old friend.

Speaking of family, my father still runs the bookstore, where he stocks a selection that's half secondhand and half new releases. Customers are invited to browse and help themselves to tea. My books stand proudly on the shelves, which is a little embarrassing. My mother is still well, too, and her younger sister, who got divorced recently, has moved in and helps out with the store.

I never dreamed it would be our family and business that would turn out, years later, to be the steadier and the more unchanged.

Even now, I sometimes look out from upstairs toward the windows of Makoto's family's home.

At the same windows, lit up behind the same trees.

Makoto's sister runs the family business now, and his brother does the bookkeeping and sales, and their customers travel from far and wide for their wagashi, which are still the pride of our town. His sister and brother each have their own children now. I imagine they have their share of troubles, but somehow they keep going as they've always done, carried downstream by the inexorable flow of time.

The same flow of time that seemed to have swallowed up Makoto's memory without a trace.

"Makoto, why do lights make you feel warm?" I asked. "When you see them at night, I mean."

It was one of our usual afternoons. He was propped against the back of the couch reading a manga. I had my head on his knee, but he didn't seem to mind its weight. He was chewing on a dry slice of pound cake my mother had baked, and the movement of his jaw transmitted itself through his knees, making my head sway in time to his chewing.

"It's not the light that's warm," Makoto said. "I'm quite sure about that."

Outside the window we could see the river, the

willow trees, and the twinkling lights of the old shops on the other side.

"But that's what it always says in books. Think of all those scenes where a person wandering in the night spots a bright window and suddenly feels homesick. And in real life, when it's late and getting dark, and you come back and see the lights are on, doesn't it make you feel safe and sound?"

I went on, "I think the lights of people's lives must just naturally feel warm."

Makoto thought for a while, and then shook his head. "*I* think the light you see comes from the people inside. The light inside them shines out, and that's where the glow really comes from. Because you can easily feel lonely even with all the lights on."

"It's the people that shine?"

"It's the light inside the people that makes it seem bright. It must be. Isn't that why you wish you could be in there with them, or feel like you want to go home?"

He's right, I thought simply. *A show house could be lit up like a chandelier and it wouldn't make you feel a thing.* I started playing with the elastic top of Makoto's sock, just to pass the time.

Even now, when I look back at these ordinary

and eternal scraps of Makoto's time in this world, when he was most at his ease, and happiest . . . I can't help but be amazed that I should have been the one at his side.

Tomo-chan's Happiness

Tomo-chan had been hoping for this for nearly five years, and now it was finally about to happen.

The person she'd liked for so long was starting to feel the same way about her.

Tomo-chan was trying to keep her cool.

But deep down inside, she didn't feel anxious at all.

The person she liked was texting her frequently and had started inviting her out to eat. *This is nice* was what she thought.

The person she liked worked for a company on a different level of her office building. Tomo-chan knew the company published a travel magazine, but because she didn't travel very much, she wasn't very interested in the magazine.

Tomo-chan did admin and odd jobs at a small design firm and always had the radio playing at her desk. When she heard a song she liked, she bought the CD from a music store nearby and played it a few times in the car on her way home. She'd try singing along, too, in her high, slightly reedy voice. Doing this would bring back all kinds of memories, so she'd go and park by the riverbank nearby, to sit quietly and listen to the sound of insects for a while.

This kind of stillness had always been very important for Tomo-chan.

She'd recently heard a song about a dragon named Puff that had been popular some time ago. Whenever she listened to it, Tomo-chan felt so strongly for poor Puff, abandoned and forgotten by Jackie, that she found herself starting to cry—and not just so her eyes would brim with tears, but she'd weep and sob enough that she usually tried to avoid thinking about the song at all.

Tomo-chan's heart took her on so many journeys over the course of its movements and fluctuations that she didn't feel the need to travel. If she joined friends for a trip to a hot spring, she might notice the change of scenery, but that was all. She'd had two relationships so far, and both had petered out because she was such a homebody. Her boyfriends came away almost impressed by how stubbornly she stuck to her unremarkable habits, and also how they could never tell what she was thinking.

For most people, being raped, even once, would be enough to make them wary of men.

That wasn't true of Tomo-chan.

And even though she was only sixteen when an older boy whom she'd known since they were both kids had taken her to the river, dragged her out of his car, and violated her, Tomo-chan never came to hate that spot on the riverbank, either.

That memory paled in comparison to the breezes that blew through there, the cold texture of the weathered bench where she often sat, and the view that changed with the seasons.

She came to loathe the boy who did it, of course.

She'd already noticed as they were having a meal together that she was repulsed by the way he ate his food. *He doesn't respect it*, she thought. Tomo-chan preferred to take her time when she ate, and the way he did it—as though he was shoveling the food into a roaring void—made her shudder.

Tomo-chan and her mother had kept a small vegetable patch in their garden, so she was used to carefully preparing undersized produce, or eating green beans three meals a day, and she hated to throw out even a shriveled potato or a daikon top. So it stood to reason that she found the boy very unlikable. But out of some momentary lapse of judgment, or maybe an uncharacteristic burst of curiosity, she had gone with him. At sixteen, being alone with a boy was new and exciting, and while hearing about the kinds of things he thought about was slightly tedious in some ways, it was also very interesting. She was also fascinated by the unfamiliar shapes of his neck and hands. That was why she got in his car.

Of course she knew that men and women had sex, having seen it in movies and so on, but what she learned was that if you didn't like the other person, it wasn't at all enjoyable, only sickening and humiliating. *But I put myself in this position*, she thought, lying still and trying to make sense of it.

Tomo-chan wasn't religious, but by nature she was very good at believing. As the disgusting wetness spread between her legs, she thought, over and over: *He did this to me against my will. He abused his power as a man. Who knows what will happen to him now?*

And although there was no ill intent in her words, nonetheless, they acted as a pure and powerful curse.

As she was leaving, she said to him, in an oddly cold voice, "I hope something extraordinary comes your way."

The following week, the boy got in a traffic accident that left the bones of his hands and feet in pieces and crushed one of his testicles. He was hospitalized for half a year.

Six months a pop, Tomo-chan thought, and this, too, seemed to make sense to her, in some unknowable way.

How Tomo-chan had fallen in love with Misawa-san, the person she liked, was a mystery even to her.

She had often seen him in the café on the first floor of their office building. Misawa-san was around forty, tall and slim, already considerably bald, and had hairy fingers. Which was to say he didn't come across as handsome at all. But Tomo-chan couldn't keep her eyes off him. When she looked at him, something dashing seemed to rise out of him that spoke far more loudly to her than the way he looked.

Tomo-chan tended to move slowly.

It took two years for her to start making eye contact with him and nodding when they met.

And in any case, Misawa-san often met his girlfriend for lunch.

Seeing them together pained Tomo-chan's heart. The two of them looked very close. Misawa-san's girlfriend was pretty, though not a great beauty, and tall like him, and had good posture and big round eyes with long lashes. She seemed quiet and composed. She and Misawa-san smiled at each other even when they didn't have much to say.

I bet they're going to get married. That's nice, Tomo-chan thought.

It is perhaps worth mentioning about Tomo-chan's character that because she saw the two of them were happy together, it never occurred to her to picture herself coming between them.

It simply transpired that she and Misawa-san saw each other often enough that they naturally started to acknowledge each other, which was a development that was quite welcome to Tomo-chan.

Tomo-chan also had an almost compulsive aversion to taking something that wasn't rightfully hers.

Her father had walked out on Tomo-chan and her mother after falling in love with another woman. This woman was his secretary and had spent a lot of time in their home. At first, she had seemed unassuming, and was kind to Tomo-chan, and considerate and helpful to her mother.

But before they knew it, the secretary was the one cooking dinner for Tomo-chan's father in the small kitchen at his office, where he often stayed late working on his interior design business, and eating with him. Tomo-chan even heard she had started taking cooking lessons just for this. She called up every night claiming to have work to discuss, and when Tomo-chan's father stayed home sick with a cold she personally brought him a basket of fruit, and when Tomo-chan and her parents planned to visit her grandmother out of town, some urgent work always came in at the last minute and kept her father from joining them.

"Some people can't resist trying to take what doesn't belong to them," Tomo-chan's mother would laugh, back when she still had the upper hand.

One winter her father broke his leg on a company ski trip and had to go to the hospital. Tomo-chan and her mother flew to Hokkaido only to find the secretary pressing her young body up against his, crying dramatically. She had taken his hand and was rubbing it against her cheek.

"Don't cry," he murmured to her, clearly besotted. "It's only a broken leg."

How is this happening? Tomo-chan wondered. *Mom and I—we rushed up here—with all his favorite food to cheer him up—but now we're just standing here with our mouths haning open. Can it really look like she cares more than we do? And if the answer is no, then why can't he see through it?*

Tomo-chan had seen the secretary earlier, downstairs in the cafeteria opposite the hospital's reception desk. She'd been smoking a cigarette while digging into a plate of omurice and breezily chatting away on her phone. Tomo-chan was amazed at the difference in her demeanor between then and now, the suddenness of the transformation. No one could say her distress wasn't genuine. It was just that there was definitely something vulgar about it, too.

"Please forgive me for crying. I was so worried about him, I couldn't help myself," the secretary said.

"Your dedication to your job is admirable,"

Tomo-chan's mother said curtly. Tomo-chan loved her for that. She loved her, and as that feeling of love welled up, she gave her mother's hand a squeeze. There in that hospital room, the two of them were like ships that had run aground and had nowhere to go.

Tomo-chan took a lesson from that intolerable scene at the hospital. She vowed: *I'm going to find a man with a warm heart. Someone who'd never fall for such a cheap trick. There must be someone out there like that.*

It might have been a particular conversation she overheard between Misawa-san and his girlfriend that first made Tomo-chan like him.

"Between my dying dog and work? Of course the dog comes first—the company's not going anywhere. I take my work seriously the rest of the time, so they can't possibly think less of me for it."

It seemed that Misawa-san had taken two days of leave to be with his dog on its deathbed.

"I think you're absolutely right," his girlfriend said. She nodded slowly.

"I mean, we got Shishimaru when I was still in

college. I'd have regretted it forever if I hadn't been there for him at the end," Tomo-chan heard Misawa-san say.

They're a nice couple, Tomo-chan thought again. But rather than feeling jealous, or even envious, she was thinking about finding someone like that for herself.

Perhaps no man could help feeling drawn to a younger body when it threw itself at him. But the fact that Tomo-chan's father got dragged all the way into marrying the secretary was entirely on him.

Tomo-chan's mom didn't immediately grant him a divorce. She said she'd give it three years, and divorce him if he hadn't come back by then.

In the meantime the secretary had Tomo-chan's father's baby. She must have dedicated every last drop of her mental energy to befuddling and bamboozling him in order to make this happen, and most likely given herself a headache in the process.

"Who are you trying to impress?" Tomo-chan had asked her the last time they met. Her mom had decided she didn't feel up to facing the woman, so

Tomo-chan had gone instead to hand over the divorce notice that her mom had finally signed.

Tomo-chan didn't have a lot of friends, but she did treasure many things: her coworkers, her parents, her pet parakeet, her pothos plants, romantic movies . . . the list was endless. Life, for Tomo-chan, was about making sure she was neatly surrounded by all the things that were important to her.

"I've always gone after what I want. It's just who I am," the secretary said with a shrug.

She's being honest for once, Tomo-chan thought. *If only she was always like this, maybe we could have been friends.*

The baby in her belly must have made the woman speak candidly. And that was what convinced Tomo-chan to let her father go. He wanted to leave, after all. And since he naturally gravitated toward roles that enabled him to realize his ideas, perhaps her mom had always been too much the finished article for him, instead of someone he could shape—maybe it all made some kind of sense.

For some time after that, whenever an ad came on TV that had been shot in Hokkaido, Tomo-chan immediately felt nauseated, and sometimes vomited. They made her remember the way the freezing damp air had pricked her cheeks, which would take her straight back into that hospital room, and then humiliation rose inside her, hot and slow: the anguish of being trapped in a place that should have been hers—where she should have most belonged—but where she was no longer welcome.

Sometime in the spring, Misawa-san started eating lunch alone.

Tomo-chan noticed the change immediately. He looked glum and had bags under his eyes. He seemed to have lost his spark.

She thought perhaps this was the opportunity she'd been waiting for. But she also wanted to leave a hurting person be. So she gently kept her distance and waited. She wasn't sure that someone else wouldn't get to him in the meantime, but he was getting thinner before her eyes and so she told herself, *Too soon. Not yet. It would be like force-feeding a sick bird.*

She waited, not like a hawk watching its prey, but easily, like a bud that was waiting for its time to flower.

Then, one day, it happened—the coincidence she'd been waiting for.

The café was busy that day, and Tomo-chan ended up sharing a table with Misawa-san and two of his coworkers.

Misawa-san said, "I'm sorry, we're crowding you." She smiled in reply. His courtesy made her want to smile at him.

At first, Misawa-san and his coworkers, who were a couple, chatted among themselves, while Tomo-chan took tiny mouthfuls of her ground chicken on rice and reveled in her happiness. But soon the couple started making vacation plans, excluding Misawa-san, and he turned to her and *saw* her for the first time.

"Do you travel a lot for work?" Tomo-chan asked.

Misawa-san nodded.

What does it mean, she asked herself, *that I like him all the way down to his hairy fingers, and their overgrown fingernails?*

It was much like how, as a bird lover, she never found the grotesque cleft inside a parakeet's throat off-putting.

"Do you know anywhere in Hokkaido that would make me fall in love in spite of myself?" she asked.

"Sure, you could marry me and come to Otaru, my hometown! What do you say?" Misawa-san said, and laughed.

Tomo-chan felt like her heart would jump out of her chest, but Misawa-san didn't seem at all embarrassed. He just sat there with a smile on his face.

"Excuse the joke, but I did grow up in Otaru. There are lots of great places around there. Do you have something against Hokkaido?" he asked.

"I do. I went there once, and it made a bad impression."

"It can happen to the best of us. What can we do to change that? Because I think Hokkaido is wonderful."

Misawa-san smiled. It was a genuine smile that said, *Let me show you what I love about it.* Tomo-chan gave him her number, and they started to text.

The first time they went for a meal together was at a little lunch spot fifteen minutes away from their office building.

Misawa-san had taken the time to gather a briefcase full of information for Tomo-chan, including photos, past issues of his magazine, and brochures from hot spring inns.

"You'll find plenty of places to stay with great views just a short distance out of town. Are you going with your boyfriend?" Misawa-san asked.

"I really wanted to take my mom. But she passed away a little while ago, so I think it'll just be me. So she can make her peace with Hokkaido, too," Tomo-chan said.

"How did she pass?"

"She had a brain hemorrhage. It was very sudden."

That night, Tomo-chan had been at the hospital, where she had rushed as fast as she could, all alone. She wanted to call for her father. But it had been so long since she'd seen him that the man she longed for was the kind father who'd been at her side years and years ago, but who was no longer anywhere to be found. Her father now was a stranger who belonged in a different home, with a new family, and was probably spending the evening with them relaxing and watching TV.

Tomo-chan's grandma and aunt were on their way from their hometown, but wouldn't get there for a while yet. Her mom had suffered a series of seizures and had already taken her last breath by the time Tomo-chan arrived. In the emergency room, everyone around her was coming and going in a hurry. She noticed a patient who'd been brought in by ambulance getting discharged to go home with their family, and started to cry.

We should have been taking you home, too, Mom, she thought.

But she told herself that it was too late, that what had happened had happened, that she had no choice but to face it. She was outside in the hospital garden, leaning against a tree in the sheer darkness and looking upward. She saw the dark branches silhouetted prettily like lace against the dark of the sky. They were swaying. The bark of the tree's trunk was warm at her back.

Tomo-chan recalled all of this and felt like she might cry.

"I'm sorry . . . That must have been hard," Misawa-san said. "Let me help. I want to make sure your trip is just the way you want it. That makes me sound like a travel agent, but I can probably give them a run for their money when it comes to local knowledge."

Tomo-chan nodded.

Misawa-san had sturdy legs, from all that walking around he must do, traveling to different places for work, and the strength to carry around a heavy bag like it was nothing.

If I could go to Hokkaido with you, I know I'd fall in love with it. The words were in her throat, but she couldn't say them yet.

She just pictured herself saying them and flushed scarlet all over her face and neck, all the way down to her collarbones.

Now, if you'll allow me to change the subject—

Tomo-chan is not the one writing this story. That is down to a novelist who has caught occasional glimpses of her life. But this writer, too, is not writing it herself, but rather is doing it on behalf of something greater, which for our present purposes we can call God.

Every day, people all around the world direct one urgent question its way: *Why me? Why did this have to happen to me?* And well they might. God doesn't lend a hand. God didn't open Tomo-chan's dad's eyes to what he was doing, or throw down a bolt of lightning from heaven to stop her from being raped, or materialize in the hospital garden to put an arm around her shoulder when she was all alone and crying.

Nor is it certain that things will work out well for her and Misawa-san. They might head to Hokkaido together, but her small breasts and dark nipples might be a disappointment to him, or her inscrutable air of fatalism put him off. Then again, he might find that same mystique attractive to the point that they decide to get married. But even then, Tomo-chan isn't guaranteed her happily-ever-after. Even Misawa-san might someday run away with a younger woman just like her father did.

Whichever of these comes to pass, God won't lift a finger to help.

But Tomo-chan has always been watched over, albeit by powers too puny to be called gods. They offered neither compassion, nor tears, nor encouragement, but they witnessed her, all too neutrally, as she slowly built up a reserve of something important in herself.

When she watched her dad being led astray by the secretary, and felt so deeply hurt, and tossed and turned at night, they saw her small back curled tight, and the sadness in her chest. They saw the unyielding hardness of the ground beneath her when she was overpowered by the boy's desires at the riverside where they had played together as children, and her vacant, forlorn expression as she walked home on her own afterward.

Later, when her mom died, even in the dark of the night when she was more alone than she had ever been, Tomo-chan was safely held. By the velvety glow of the night, the touch of the wind as it drifts softly past, the blinking of stars, the voices of insects, and things like that.

Somewhere deep down, Tomo-chan knew this all along. And so she was never really alone.

Dead-End Memories

That day, Nishiyama and I had a picnic in a small park in the neighborhood.

Did he invite me out to get some lunch? I can't recall how exactly it happened.

I was lounging around in my room upstairs. I'd just hand-washed some laundry—out of necessity, since I'd run out of things to wear—and hung them up in a sunny spot, and sat down for a breather. That was when Nishiyama, who'd arrived to clean and prep before opening the bar, called out to me from downstairs.

"Hello? Mimi?"

"I'm up here!"

"Have you had lunch?"

"Not yet."

"Me neither. Want to grab some food?"

"Sure."

Truth be told, I was enough of a coward that I worried about bumping into those two every time I ventured out into the city, but I thought I'd be safe enough with Nishiyama. I suddenly found myself feeling eager to get outside.

I put on a jacket, and stepped out in sneakers and no makeup.

The autumn sky was transparent all the way to where it melded into the horizon, and endlessly ambivalent, with nothing definite about it anywhere. It seemed to console me gently in the limbo where I found myself suspended.

As we walked, the sun warmed me until I felt cozy and at ease.

With perfect timing, as though he'd just thought of it, Nishiyama said, "It's a nice day. Shall we eat in the park?"

So we stopped at a fast-food place opposite the park and ordered a variety of things to go. Fries, hot dogs, coffee, dessert—more than we could finish, but we got all of it wrapped up, splitting the bill, and ate on the grass.

The light was tinted gold, and the sky was miles away. The trees lining the road, retaining an exuberant echo of summer, swayed quietly in the breeze.

"You can't beat a picnic—even on a little scrap of dirt like this. Everything tastes great when you're outside," Nishiyama said, contentedly.

I loved the way he looked when he was happy. I'd always thought there was something something singular about his relationship to happiness, but I'd never been able to put my finger on it.

"Tell me, Nishiyama," I said, "what does being happy mean, for you?"

"What do you mean?" he asked. "Are we talking philosophy?"

"No, I'm talking about what you picture when you think about happiness."

"Hmm . . . What do *you* see, Mimi?"

Funny not being able to answer my own question, I thought, and waited for something to come to me.

It took a good five minutes.

In the meantime we sat in silence, side by side on the grass, legs out in front of us, eating the occasional french fry.

"I picture Doraemon, the twenty-second-century robot cat, and his friend Noby," I said.

"But that's a kids' comic!" Nishiyama said.

"I have a clock with this scene printed on its face. The two of them are in Noby's room. They're grinning, and there are books scattered all around the floor. Doraemon's sitting cross-legged, and Noby's lying on his front propped up on a folded cushion, and they're reading manga and eating dorayaki. The whole situation—their friendship, how Doraemon moves in to Noby's closet and becomes a part of the family, the comfortable Japanese middle-class domesticity—it seems like the picture of happiness," I said.

"That's just like us, then. You're literally a guest of the house," Nishiyama said, "and we're lying on warm grass, eating good food, in great company, taking it easy."

"I know. I think I might be happy right now," I said.

The feeling of being backed into a corner hadn't quite let go of me. But those days, in which I had no choice but to feel that *now* was all that existed, because if I took my eyes off the present moment the sadness would overcome me, were peculiarly happy ones for just that reason. I knew this even as I was in them. Everything I saw made me regretful, but compared with the morass of half-dead days that had preceded it, this new world, shot through with sharp sorrow as it was, had a merciful clarity.

"I think happiness, for me, is about feeling free," Nishiyama said. "When I can go anywhere and do anything, and I feel good. I sense this strength coming up from deep in my gut, and I know I can get where I want to go. It's not about *where* I go, but having the choice—that's happiness." He was looking at the sky.

It's his desire for freedom that makes him move so fluidly, and makes people feel so contented and joyful when they're around him, I thought.

I know now that just then, under the worst possible conditions, I was in the midst of my greatest happiness.

If I could take those hours from that afternoon and put them in a box, I'd treasure them for the rest of my life. Happiness descends on you suddenly, regardless of circumstance, and so indifferently that it seems cruel. It doesn't care where you are, or who you're with.

You don't see it coming.

You can't make it happen. It might arrive with your next breath, or you might never get to experience it no matter how long you wait. Like the movements of waves, or shifts in the weather, the miracle lies in wait for everyone.

I just didn't know it then.

When he was a boy, Nishiyama had practically been kept prisoner in his house by his father—a real eccentric, who was a well-known professor of British and American literature and also wrote detective novels. Nishiyama had become so severely malnourished that he nearly died.

His mother had left the family, finding life with her husband intolerable, and his father, ill-equipped to look after a child, had kept him shut in his room for nearly two years, hardly letting him leave the house. His father fed him whenever he remembered, and locked him in the house when he went out. Eventually, some relatives reported it to the police, and because he and his father lived in a remote, mountainous part of Nagano, Nishiyama ended up getting freed in a dramatic rescue operation. This was back when child abuse was just starting to be taken seriously by the media, so the story got a lot of attention and sparked a debate that went beyond the actual facts of his situation.

I remembered seeing him on the news when he got rescued. He looked dazed and uncertain, but there was a gleam in his eyes, and even a hint of hope in his expression.

"I like it out here. It's so pretty. And the leaves, they're so bright," he'd said, dreamily.

Nishiyama was removed from his father and sent to live with his aunt, who was wealthy and permissive and left him to his own devices. Suddenly, he had a life that was the total opposite of the captivity he'd suffered before.

Now, at the age of thirty, he'd ended up as the manager of Cul-de-Sac, a little place that played music and served drinks, the kind of neighborhood spot that was neither a pub nor a club, but something in between.

I was convinced that Nishiyama, growing up first confined indoors, and then cast out on his own, had discovered a secret—some powerful insight that he'd gained from learning to live with whatever fate handed him. It had to be the reason his eyes were so clear, and how he seemed to intuit things he couldn't have known.

•

Cul-de-Sac was on the first floor of what had once been a private residence at the end of a dead-end street. The building was run-down and due to be demolished soon, so Cul-de-Sac was moving to larger premises next year. Nishiyama was going to take the opportunity to go to Tokyo and train as a bartender at a well-known cocktail bar.

The owner of Cul-de-Sac was my uncle. He was taking some time off to vacation abroad before moving the bar to its new location. Meanwhile, I'd been wanting to feel as though I'd run away from home, but being the obedient daughter I actually was, I'd gotten my mom to ask him a favor and temporarily moved into the small apartment upstairs.

Cul-de-Sac was in a big city an hour away from my hometown.

The city wasn't as big as Tokyo, of course, but it was the biggest one in the region. The bullet train stopped there, and it had department stores and busy shopping districts with independent shops.

My fiancé, Takanashi, had moved here for work.

His company was headquartered in this city, and he'd been transferred from the branch office in our hometown. We'd been dating since college and had everything planned out so that we'd get married once he got a small promotion that would bring him back to our town. We'd gotten our parents' blessings, and exchanged engagement rings.

Sometime the following spring, though, Takanashi's responses to my emails and voice mails had become sporadic.

I just assumed he was very busy, and looked forward to his visits back home.

And, in fact, when he did come home for weekends, he seemed the same as usual.

We went on dates, kissed, walked hand in hand, and went out to eat like always.

Occasionally we got a hotel room, and had a nice time unwinding, catching up on each other's lives just like when we were in college.

But eventually his visits petered out, and he rarely called me back even when I left a voice mail.

Still I kept waiting, without thinking much of it. We'd been together for long enough that it didn't seem like a big deal.

When I didn't hear from him for long enough that I mentioned it to his elder sister and brother, he'd call me not too long after, like they must have told him to. And so things kept limping along.

The first time I suspected something was

amiss—as belated as it seems, even to me—was last summer, when he didn't come home even once. Our hometown was on the coast, and he loved swimming in the sea, and when he stayed away all summer I thought for the first time there must be something wrong.

Looking back, it's kind of incredible how nonchalant I'd been about the whole thing, but maybe on some level I'd actually known. A sigh used to escape my lips every time I looked at the sky, and when I got a little drunk, tears would well up for no reason I could think of.

But I was living at home with my mom, my dad, and my sister, and each day had its share of bustle and drama and surprises, and on top of that I was busy helping at my mom's sandwich stall nearly every day, and having fun, too, so time kind of slipped by.

On my days off I sometimes took the family car and went out to the coast.

Most of my memories of Takanashi and me were at the beach, so the sandy shore, in the approach to fall, felt especially lonely.

But my memories kept me warm. Things we'd said, the ways our personalities complemented each other, times we drove around playing CDs we'd bought or borrowed and cried at great songs. How, after we went long-distance, we'd hold hands every chance we got, not wanting to let each other go. Long conversations about what our lives would be like once we were married, when we wanted to have kids, and where we could see ourselves living. Swimming in the sea every summer. Spotting fish in the water, or going out to the rocks to find shells and jellyfish. Lighting bonfires on the shore. All these memories put a smile on my face every time I looked back on them.

"I'm thinking of giving him a surprise visit," I said to my sister one day.

We were up late, talking and polishing off the day's leftover sandwiches.

"Hmm . . . I just hope you don't end up getting hurt," she said. "I mean, he hasn't reached out because he doesn't want to, right? Do you think it might be best to let it fade out?"

My sister had been coming out with some pretty grown-up opinions lately, in spite of being younger by five years.

She was eating a fruit sandwich, and her mouth was making exactly the same shapes as it had when she was a baby, but there was a gravity to the words that now came out of it.

"Isn't the whole point of being engaged to stop us from breaking up by accident like that?" I said. "It's supposed to be a commitment."

"Sure, but the reality is that you haven't heard from him. I mean, we know you can be slow on the uptake sometimes—are you sure you haven't missed something? If you're happy with things the way they are, fair enough, but otherwise, I think it's time you put an end to it. As your sister, it's upsetting to think of you going off and getting married to someone who doesn't treat you right," she said.

"Takanashi used to say he liked what a dope I am. That it was good I did my own thing, and never went to mixers or cared about being popular at college. Anyway, I think he's probably really busy with work. He feels secure enough in our relationship that he thinks he can call me whenever he wants, you know?"

As I was telling her this, I thought of Takanashi's face again, and felt my heart ache.

Takanashi, my kind, good-looking, charismatic,

well-rounded boyfriend. Takanashi, who always put our relationship first, even though he sometimes went out with female friends. The sweet journey of our four years together, when he called me every day and we never missed a weekend date.

"If he's doing that now, what does that mean for how he'll act in the future? Everyone says a man's priorities change once he starts his career," my sister said.

"I'm starting to think you're right. Do you really think I should give up on him?"

"To be honest, it's painful watching you waiting around when he's been doing his best to ghost you for so long," she said.

"I guess I think of it less like waiting around, and more like not dwelling on it? I keep wanting to believe that things are actually okay. So maybe I need to go see with my own eyes where we stand. Meet him in person one last time and end it."

"Do you really think you'd do it?" My sister looked genuinely surprised.

"I might be naive, but I'm twenty-five and a grown adult—I can take care of myself," I said.

But I also couldn't bear the thought of not seeing him one last time.

Deep down, I was hoping that if I went to him,

he'd take me in his arms and say, *Mimi, I'm sorry. I've had so much on my plate. It's great to see you.*

"Shall I come with you for backup?" my sister asked.

"Don't worry, I'll be fine. I'm supposed to be the older one. Just give Mom some help with the stall while I'm gone."

"Of course. But promise me: if it turns out to be a disaster, don't do anything stupid. Call me first."

When did she become so grown-up? I wondered. We'd been doing this for years now—spending time late into the night sharing food, bickering, and talking about our relationships. Somewhere along the way, she'd become not just my sister, but a friend.

On nights when we were both home, one of us would poke a head around the other's door. We both looked forward to unwinding at the end of the day, provisioned with sandwiches, beer, tea, and snacks. There was something inviting and warm about a bedroom at night with the TV on. It was a place where all the loneliness and fear of the world outside seemed to melt away.

Until recently, the two of us had used to talk about how we'd miss our chats once I was married, but now it was beginning to seem like we'd be here until she went off to be a bride.

When the two of us were together, I could pretend I was still a child. Confiding in her almost made me lose sight of how this problem was mine alone to deal with, even if she was family.

I knew it'd take me a while to get over Takanashi, however things turned out. My mind simply wasn't built to let things go quickly. I already tended to have to take my time over things compared with other people even at the best of times.

I'd never been the kind of woman who needed a man to complete her life, so Takanashi was special. He could get under my skin, cause me sorrow, and bring me deep joy. That was how our relationship worked: he was always in action, while I stayed put and accepted what I was given. Things just always seemed to work out that way.

At home with my family, I tried to live up to the role of the eldest child, if in my own ponderous way. Perhaps Takanashi had been the only person in my life I'd really let myself depend on.

In the end, things turned out even worse than I'd feared.

I sent Takanashi three messages saying I wanted

to talk to him, without mentioning I was coming to visit. Then I left the same message on his voice mail, twice.

"Whatever's going on, I'd like to speak to you. We can't move on with things up in the air like this. I think we should sort it out. Let's just meet and talk things through," I said, trying not to sound too pathetic.

But he still didn't respond.

So I packed a bag for a three-day trip, just in case, and took the train to the town where Takanashi lived.

I checked into a business hotel near the station and waited for night.

To tell the truth, even as I dropped my bags and went out on my own to have some lunch, some part of me was excited. *I get to see his face tonight. And once we're together, he'll remember about us, and get back to his old self. We'll talk about everything, and be just as close as we used to be.* I felt happy simply knowing he was somewhere in this city. Even just the possibility that he might have once eaten lunch at the restaurant where I was sitting made me long for him.

I went back to my hotel and took a nap, and had a sad dream.

In the dream, I was walking through some unknown town, alone and lost. The streets felt uncertain underfoot, and when I asked people the way they wouldn't answer, or I couldn't make out a word of what they said. The air was a milky rainbow haze, and I was beset by an unidentifiable melancholy that made it impossible to think.

At 9 p.m., I set out for Takanashi's.

This was his new apartment, where, for some reason, I'd never been invited.

I spotted his car in the parking lot opposite the building.

The lights were on, and I could see someone was home. Reassured, I rang the doorbell.

A woman came to the door. She was pretty, in a sophisticated kind of way, and seemed like the capable type—nothing like me. I noticed with dismay that she also resembled Takanashi's mother.

"Are you looking for Jin? He's not home yet," she said.

I stuttered. "So, I'm . . . My name is Mimi Yokoyama, and Takanashi's . . . I'm actually his fiancée," I said, at least going through the motions of laying claim to my superior position, in spite of it being pretty obvious I was already at a huge disadvantage given how I was calling him by his last name, like we were still kids at school.

"Oh . . . He's told me about you. Please, come in," she said.

She was dressed in jeans and a T-shirt, with her hair in a ponytail, and had evidently been in the middle of cooking dinner. When I looked around the room, it was plain to see she was the one who had decorated it and kept it tidy, and that they lived here together. No photographs of me, no mementos of us, and about the only thing I recognized was his suit on a clothes hanger. He'd worn it a lot back when he lived in our hometown. *I know that suit,* I thought. Even that was enough to almost make me burst into tears.

"In the beginning, I thought I could just be his lover here in the city," she said, putting on some water for tea.

I started to feel dizzy, as though the room were spinning.

"But as time went on, we found out how much we had in common, and . . . Jin always said, *Give me time. Mimi's such a romantic, she won't take it well.* Then my parents and his mom found out we were living together, and we decided to make it official. I'm sorry. I didn't realize you didn't know."

"I'm sorry? What exactly—"

"We're getting married this winter. His work's going well, and the company granted his request to stay at the head office, so we'll be here for the foreseeable future."

"You're joking," I said, weakly. Talk about a bolt from the blue, I thought. I'd been too absorbed in thinking about what was going on for me—no wonder, since my name was Mimi—that I'd missed what had been going on the whole time. I was so thoroughly caught off guard that my brain was grasping at the most nonsensical of explanations.

I couldn't even cry; only laugh at what a fool I'd been, how I'd rushed around doing things like piping embarrassing messages into his voice mail and asking his siblings for advice, not knowing I was already old news.

Just then, to make a bad situation even worse, we heard Takanashi at the door.

"I'm home," he called out, and came in.

He was home . . . here. This was his home. *Their* home.

Takanashi saw the two of us sitting across the table from each other, looked taken aback, and then seemed to grasp the situation.

"Sorry, Mimi. I was going to make things right come winter. I still care about you—I've just found someone I love more. I've made my decision," he said, so innocently that I couldn't find it in me to hate him. He looked really upset.

It was too much for me to take. Tears rolled down my cheeks, and I wanted to say something, but I couldn't find the words. The best I could manage was to say, "Well, if that's how things are, there's nothing I can do. I understand."

I walked out of their cozy, brightly lit apartment into the night, alone.

I'm not sure how long I wandered the streets. At one point I stopped at a bar and had three cocktails. A man sitting next to me kept trying to strike up a conversation, but the bar staff noticed how distracted I was and intervened, and he left me alone eventually. Then, wanting to cool my tipsy head, I went back out into the city. This hateful city, where everyone had a place they belonged and an enviable life, and I had no one.

How did I end up here? I wondered. My life up

till now had gone according to plan—I had a loving family, I'd finished college, and I'd gotten engaged.

At the same time, another part of me was thinking, *Out in the wide world, people go through this kind of thing all the time.*

It wasn't until I was back at the hotel and under a hot shower that the tears really came. *It was already over,* I thought, *I just didn't know it.*

My sister had called multiple times and left voice mails. I was still crying, but I called her back.

"I knew it," she said, "I knew it—Mimi, you dummy, you total idiot. You're too soft for your own good." But I could hear she was crying, too. "Get back here soon so we know you're okay," she said, multiple times.

I, too, felt concerned at my own stupidity.

I did know, I thought. *But if I knew, then why did I come this far . . . ?* I felt like I'd woken up from a dream.

Part of me wanted to go home. Pick up my life just as it had been and forget all about this. Although my cherished vision of life with Takanashi had gone up in smoke, I wanted to bury myself inside the comfort of life in a family where I belonged. But something also told me that going home right now would mean destroying some aspect of myself in a way that would be subtle, but irreversible.

I'd been clinging to the idea of being engaged, the promise of joy and stability it represented. The idea had the power to make everyone take for granted that it was a happy, sure thing.

I felt ashamed at having treasured it all this time, when in actuality it had already long since crumbled away to nothing.

He's my fiancé, I'd told myself, and convinced myself there was no way there could be anything wrong. I'd been lying to myself.

I woke with puffy eyelids and no idea where I was. Then it all came back to me, and I groaned.

My days of subsisting on old memories like they were hard candy were over.

I used to wake up every morning and wonder what Takanashi would be up to that day. But that part of my life was finished. He'd turned into someone whose life had nothing to do with mine.

So what now? I thought, looking up at the blank ceiling of my hotel room.

Whatever the answer was, I knew I wasn't ready to go back to my old life.

I picked up the phone, called my mom and dad, and told them the whole story.

Understandably, they were furious, and wanted to go and talk things over with Takanashi's parents. I told them it didn't really make a difference to me as long as the engagement was called off. I also said it was really for the best, since I'd grown tired of him, too—which was a lie.

Although I knew it was out of concern for me, this outpouring of emotion made me even less inclined to go home, so I told them I'd stay in the city for a bit to cool my head. Both they and my sister were against it, but I dreaded the train journey, and felt like I'd rather die than face their pity back home.

My bedroom walls were still covered with photos of cherished moments, and there were gifts, diaries, too many things that would remind me of him. I wasn't ready to face those, either.

Plus, I trusted that if I gave them time, my mom, at least, would simmer down and realize that making a fuss over this only made things more difficult for me.

I knew I was fortunate to have my family's love, and always had been.

My mom, my sister, and I worked alongside one another like three sisters at the sandwich stall my mom ran as a hobby during the day—a modest but friendly kind of place—and my dad worked an office job and was dependable and put family first. For the moment things were stable for us, and all was well.

There was nothing wrong with that.

But I saw now that being part of such a tight-knit family could at times be a burden. If I couldn't be on my own, this pain would never begin to heal. I was the one who'd been in love with Takanashi, so the hurt was mine. I wanted to honor that, even just for a short time.

In the end, they agreed it would put their minds at rest if I'd stay in the empty apartment above the bar my uncle owned in the city. *Just a week or two*, I promised them—*I'll get myself together and then I'll come home. I'll call every day, I won't do anything stupid.*

For the first time ever, I was living away from home, and my time was wholly my own.

I reflected on things at my leisure. In the mornings I would wake up and stay in bed, looking out the window and picturing Takanashi somewhere out there under the same blue sky. The thought still filled some part of me with a nostalgic happiness, which made me want to cry. I felt like a fool.

But it was true: I'd missed him for so long that the sheer fact that he was alive was comfort to me.

You were lucky to have been with—and gotten engaged to—the first person you really loved, I tried to tell myself. *This kind of thing happens all the time to people. It must have been hard for her, too, having to sneak around for so long when they wanted to be together. So we're even*, I thought, and wept.

After I moved in upstairs, Nishiyama started checking on me every so often. My uncle had probably asked him to keep an eye on me, just in case. Nishiyama arrived at the bar every afternoon to clean or prep before opening in the evening.

At first I'd just call back to him from under the covers, like a snail, but after the third day or so I started to feel more at ease with him. It was a purely practical relationship where we didn't have to exchange any more words than were necessary, and that suited me very well.

Eventually, I started feeling like I owed him something. I decided to express my appreciation by lending a hand in the bar when it seemed busy.

I don't know whether I was actually helping or just getting in the way, but Nishiyama seemed happy to let me work, presumably because he knew what I was going through. So I just tried to make myself useful as quietly and unobtrusively as I could.

I hung back from talking to the customers and spent a lot of time observing the interactions that took place around Nishiyama.

The regulars all adored him. It was as though they came in just to see him.

And, like them, I found myself drawn to his friendliness and positivity, the aura of kindness that he carried around with him, the way he made everyone feel welcome and put me in mind of a breeze coming off the ocean on a sunny day.

When I was around him, I felt more free, somehow.

Maybe the comparison was unoriginal, but Nishiyama was like a bird flying off into the sunset, gathering speed with every beat of his powerful wings. The air he moved through was wind on his face, and he looked down at the world from a great height—that was how he seemed to me.

It was common knowledge that Nishiyama rarely turned anyone down, but also didn't linger. He didn't have a steady girlfriend, and everyone knew he was always dating several women. His position was that he liked them all, but none more than the next. He was up-front about this, and the fact that he didn't have a phone and could be hard to get hold of also meant that none of the women he dated could ever get too close.

Because of all this, some people envied my proximity to him, but I was in no place to make anything of it. I had problems of my own to deal with and no room to spare worrying about what people were saying. The bar just happened to be my uncle's business, and besides, I was leaving soon.

Customers sometimes got jealous or angry with him, too. Both men and women tried to lecture him. His very elusiveness seemed to make people want to find some way to involve themselves in his life.

To me, it looked like this was who Nishiyama really was. People read all kinds of things into his actions precisely because the rest of us were rarely able to live that way.

I can't deny I was drawn to him physically. He moved gracefully in a way we all found captivating. His looks weren't anything out of the ordinary, but his eyes twinkled like diamonds, and his thin lips and tall nose and the slight wave to his hair gave him an appealing look.

That said, for me just then—freshly devastated by a relationship that wasn't even a workplace romance or a secret affair, but in which I'd felt incredibly trapped nonetheless—I think it was Nishiyama's philosophy, or way of living, that I was most attracted to.

All the more so, I think, because I didn't have romantic feelings for him.

The thought of Takanashi out there somewhere under the same sky, living happily ever after with someone who wasn't me, still sent pangs of pain through me every day. The two of them were living the life that I should have had with him: Takanashi carrying her bags for her if they were heavy, her cooking curry and serving it with pickled shallots instead of cucumbers, just the way he liked.

As much as it hurt to dwell on these scenes in

my mind, heartbroken and alone, even this was probably a necessary part of my healing.

"I think I'm pretty good at adjusting to new environments, taking things as they come," Nishiyama said. We were in the bar having coffee before locking up and going home.

"But after what happened when you were young, there must be some things you find, I don't know, difficult, or unbearable," I said.

"Are you asking out of curiosity?" he said.

"Curiosity, and also not wanting to do anything to upset you while I'm here," I said.

He smiled. "I guess I still don't really like things that remind me of feeling cornered. Some women give off that vibe, and it turns me off. People who want to be with you all the time? Really not my type."

"I can see how that must be," I said. "But why is it that everyone wants you?"

"I think it's because I can take care of myself. Having to be inside all the time as a kid, and then being too free after that, I saw the upsides and downsides of both, so I've found my balance, I guess. And

I've learned not to have illusions about things. My dad wasn't abnormal, he just got the balance wrong. My life wasn't as crazy as the media made it sound. My dad and I, we were more like a widower scientist and a little kid out in the wilderness, just doing our best to survive. They made a big deal about me being malnourished, but my dad was pretty skinny, too. He'd forget to eat whenever he got absorbed in an idea. He's a strange man, but I still see him once in a while, and we get along okay. Being pitied by everyone afterward was way worse. I thought, *What the hell do they know about it?* People suddenly started acting like they understood me just because I'd been through something unusual that they automatically assumed was tragic."

"So that's why you prefer to keep people at a distance. Still, you must be sorry this place is closing. It's a great bar, and you've got so many regulars."

"I am a little. But my life in Tokyo will be a new adventure."

"I get sad just imagining life without our little sandwich stall. Never seeing our customers again! I'd worry about the doddery old lady who gets her grandkids fruit sandwiches every day—I could cry just thinking about it."

"That sounds idyllic. It must be nice to live like that."

"I've just been spoiled. Plus, I was in an environment where my staying like a child made people happy." *Takanashi also found my inexperience reassuring,* I thought to myself.

"You don't have to apologize about having had a stable upbringing. It's a strength you have—you should use it. You can go back to your hometown and fall in love again. Make a good match, see your parents regularly, stay close with your sister, and build your community. You have the power to do that. That's your destiny, and you don't need to justify it to anyone. *He's* the one that's been ejected from *your* life."

"It's a relief to hear you say that. I was starting to think I got into this mess because there was something wrong with the way I live. But all those things you said, they're exactly what I want—that's what happiness is for me. That's never going to change. So when I'm ready, I'll go home and start living for myself again."

"That's it. If you thought you could pack up and go make a better life somewhere else right now, *that* would be tempting fate. Each one of us has our own personal rock bottom. There are so many people out there with lives far less fortunate than ours, and if we got even a taste of what it's like to be them it would crush us, we'd never make it through. Because we're lucky, we've got things pretty easy. But that's not something we need to feel ashamed of."

Nishiyama was delivering hard truths that belied his smile, but it didn't bother me at all. I knew he was right.

"Being born into my family and having their support now—I think of it as a privilege, and also my duty. It might sound kind of mystical, but I feel like I *chose* to be born to them. I'm just taking a little break right now. Everyone needs that sometimes."

"Good, you get it. That's totally okay. I'd feel responsible if you went off the rails now, you know? But you're stronger than I thought, you've got your head screwed on right. That's what you get from growing up in a good family, I guess," he said, smiling again.

"I feel pathetic, and humiliated, and I almost hate myself over this whole thing sometimes. But I'm not going to turn my back on the life I've lived so far just because of it," I said.

I was struck again by the scope of Nishiyama's

perspective. Not to mention his amazing ability to express and share what he was thinking.

I'm not quite sure how to put this, but it was almost as though—because Nishiyama had already come through the hardest times of his life—the gods had granted him a kind of grace in the form of permission to simply enjoy the remainder of it.

His sheer presence made a room feel warmer, made me feel like I'd been blessed. I understood exactly why people wanted to be near him, like he was some kind of talisman: *Keep Nishiyama with you, and fortune will be on your side! Find refuge from the anxieties and uncertainties of this world.*

I knew firsthand that after talking to him, about any old thing, I didn't feel lonely at all.

My body felt more at ease, my thoughts happier. I felt like life might yet have good things in store for me. And it wasn't a heady, unmoored feeling, but a quiet, rolling wave.

This feels good, I thought. *I'm just happy he's here. I don't need him to be mine.* I wanted to appreciate him the way I did giant trees in the park, which gave people shelter and relief but didn't belong to anybody.

Since I'd always assumed he was something to

be shared, to me he was akin to cake, or a hot spring, or good music, a steady presence I could rely on to be there when I needed to catch my breath.

One night at the bar, during a lull between customers, I was doing my best impression of a goat, scarfing down the stew Nishiyama had cooked for our dinner, when, out of nowhere, he said, "Mimi, is there another reason why you're holding on to things? Aside from regrets?"

I was caught off guard, and the truth came tumbling out of my mouth. "He still owes me money."

How had I let it slip? I hadn't breathed a word to anyone—not my parents or my sister, or anyone else in my family, or his parents, or his new girlfriend. I'd pledged never to bring it up ever again.

I was surprised at myself. Then I realized that I'd wanted to tell him.

Oh—I want someone to know how I feel, I thought. *I want someone to comfort me. That's how small a person I am.*

Tears rose to my eyes.

Nishiyama looked concerned. "How much are we talking about?" he said.

"A mi—a million yen," I said.

His eyes went wide. "How'd that happen? It doesn't seem like the kind of money you'd lend to someone you were engaged to."

"I was keeping it for when we got married. For furniture and things, just so we had a buffer. Everything I'd saved up since I was a kid—all my New Year's gifts, and money from part-time work and things. I lent it to him when he bought his car. We were going to share it, anyway. I went to buy it with him, went on the test drive and everything," I said, feeling more and more dejected as I went on.

"Mimi, you idiot," Nishiyama said.

"The money's not the reason I'm feeling stuck," I said. "I don't want to ask him for it back. But I realized just now that I've been feeling wronged, and I needed to get it off my chest. Please don't tell anyone. And definitely not my uncle. He'd get straight on the phone to my mom. Things are bad enough as they are." He didn't look at me or say a word. "I'm done dwelling on it. What I want right now is to *be* here, just like this . . ."

. . . *like a jellyfish drifting on the current, in the transparent tint of a sky moving through autumn into winter, in this city where I'm no one at all.*

I wiped my tears.

"Don't be stupid. That money is yours!"

"I *am* an idiot, that's how I got into this mess. Forget it. Or *you* do it, then. If you can get it back from him then you can keep it."

"This is what I hate about people who've never been broke. Don't say 'a million' like it's nothing. People skip town for less than that," he said, as if I were his kid sister.

It's fine, I wanted to say. *I just needed someone to know. Thanks for being here for me.*

But instead, I changed the subject. "How about a cup of tea? I'll put the kettle on."

"A customer brought in some cakes yesterday," Nishiyama said.

"Sounds great."

He peered into the refrigerator under the bar. "Looks like cheesecake, strawberry shortcake, or caramel flan—which would you like?"

"Strawberry shortcake for me."

"You got it."

"What kind of tea do you want? Green tea?"

"Sounds good."

I put the water on to boil.

Now that the catch in my chest had been lifted,

everything looked brighter, and the tea and cake tasted brand-new, as if I were having both for the very first time.

I really needed to tell someone, huh. It was important to me, I thought. I was still amazed at myself.

Nishiyama, in his kindness, didn't revisit the topic.

"This flan's really sweet!"

"Are you sure it isn't a crème brûlée?"

"What's the difference?"

"The burnt caramel on top?"

"Is that right . . ."

Our sporadic conversation punctuated the peaceful moment we shared while we waited for our next customers, and I felt my distress quietly ebbing away.

To tell the truth, I'd thought about the loan several times before, and it had left a bitter taste in my mouth each time.

I wasn't hurting for money—I had other savings, and I was getting a little from working at the sandwich stall. I'd often used the car when Takanashi and I had still been in touch, and the plan had always been that it would eventually be ours. Besides, he'd almost always paid when we went on dates, and my engagement ring hadn't been inexpensive, either, and it was still in my wallet even though I probably should have given it back.

Sometimes when I felt mean I thought about asking him to pay me back. *But what if the reason he held back from talking to me about breaking up wasn't out of love, or regret, or kindness, but only because he wasn't in a position to give me the money if I asked?* I never let myself take that train of thought any further, terrified by the possibility of getting any more hurt than I already was.

It's not like his repaying me is going to bring back what we had. Then again, if I had that money I could at least take my sister on a nice vacation somewhere . . . My thoughts kept going in circles.

Asking for it back would have meant getting to see him again.

Maybe he's having second thoughts. Maybe, if we meet up face-to-face, we'll be able to work things out . . . The ray of hope I felt at the idea made me feel even more pathetic.

The thing about money was that by the time you

started thinking this way, it had already turned into something imaginative, rather than anything real.

When I pictured being able to use it to go abroad with my sister, the money glowed orange in my mind, and when I made it into an excuse to see him one last time, it felt dingy and tainted. If I thought of it as something he had intentionally taken from me, my resentment at his betrayal turned my heart even darker, and I felt like the victim, and it turned the swampy color of recrimination.

If the same amount of money could take on different colors, I'd of course prefer to choose only the pleasant ones. But I knew things didn't work that way. I had the sense I was merely looking on at the wheel of colors inside me as it spun around of its own accord.

It struck me that family, work, friendships, engagements—all of these were like spiderwebs placed to protect people from the more distressing colors that lurked within themselves. The more safety nets you had under you, the less far you had to fall, and if you were lucky you might live your entire life without even noticing what was below.

Didn't every parent want to protect their child

from finding out how far down the bottom was? It made sense, then, that my mom and dad seemed to be more concerned about my situation than I was. They were worried I might keep falling.

That's why humans developed ways of working together; to survive, to make sure nobody falls between the cracks . . . My ideas expanded to a grand scale, and suddenly the thought of people living covered in dog poo on the streets of India, or people racking up debts to loan sharks and having to run away in the middle of the night, alcoholics breaking their families apart, stressed single mothers mistreating their children, wives murdering their bullying mothers-in-law—all these lives stopped seeming like dark and heavy stories that I wanted to avert my eyes from.

There, above a little bar called Cul-de-Sac, like some callow undergraduate, I mused: *Maybe this has been a good thing after all. What I'm going through is only like being perched on a soft cloud and peering through a small gap at other people's lives. But who's to say whether I'm looking up or down? The important thing is that I'm choosing to keep my eyes open* . . .

Because what you choose to pay attention to defines your world. That was the conclusion I came to.

Suddenly, Takanashi felt very distant from me, and for the first time, I was able to think of him not as an ideal hand warmly grasping mine, but as a complete stranger, with values totally different from me.

For one thing, if I'd met someone else and fallen in love, I would have told him immediately.

You could say that the fact he'd brought about this whole situation by not doing so meant we were incompatible on a fairly fundamental level.

Having all these thoughts filling my head felt almost soothing, like I was young again.

In years past, I'd looked up at the night sky and aimlessly pondered big questions like the meaning of life and death, or what kind of person I wanted to be.

On those nights the stars twinkled, and the sky looked infinitely far away.

The bite of the wind, the sense of a vast future unfolding before me, the scent of the tide that filled my hometown—all of these things came back to me vividly.

I felt like I had it in me to go after that feeling again: that state of mind in which my heart expanded freely, limitlessly, like music, like a song. It was as though the calloused outer layer of my heart, dulled to pain from years of routine, had peeled off. Sure, it hurt more now, but the air I could feel on my skin was a lot more invigorating than the numbness that had been there before.

Okay, I'm ready. Time to get back and start again.

My one regret was having to say goodbye to Nishiyama. But he'd already helped me so much, and I'd learned a lot, and I assumed our paths would surely cross again at some point.

"I'm going home. It's time," I said to Nishiyama as I walked into the bar.

"No way! I'll miss you!" he said, sounding genuinely disappointed. "Don't take this the wrong way, but it's been real fun having you here."

"I've enjoyed it, too," I said. "I almost wish I could stay forever."

The bar was still empty, and I was polishing the glassware. I knew my uncle had built up his collection one by one over the years, so keeping them gleaming seemed like the least I could do.

He hadn't been in touch at all during the time I'd been here, and for his kindness I was truly grateful. Left to my own devices, I hadn't needed to worry about repaying his generosity in any way until the next time I planned to visit, probably around New Year, when I could thank him properly. If he'd been around, he would have wanted to take me out and cheer me up, and I probably would have felt smothered and obligated. *I was free here because I was among strangers*, I thought, and felt nostalgic about my time here already.

I'd been nobody, working for nothing, but I had Nishiyama looking out for me, and a bed to retreat to when I got tired. I'd been free to think things over to my heart's content without anyone interrupting me, or to put on more makeup than usual without anyone knowing the difference, or to cry my eyes out without anyone commenting on how puffy they looked afterward. Just by walking around the city, I could immediately take on the part of a traveler. The words I read in books seemed to strike me more deeply, and with my senses sharpened by grief, I noticed the glittering transition of the seasons as clearly as if I held the grief in the palm of my hand. It had been a long while since I'd experienced a fall so clear and crisp.

Through all this I'd always had a home to go back to. I'd only been playing at the blues. I'd learned I could be surprisingly spiteful, and stingy with money, and as ignorant and overtrusting and immature as I'd suspected.

I was sure that the things I'd seen in my short time here—days viewed only through a lens of grief, as through the bottom of a glass—had been firmly etched into my memory, and would serve me well wherever I went. Because of that, I felt ready to let go, as though I were coming to the end of a long voyage.

I was truly glad that I'd stuck it out in this city.

"When are you leaving? Don't say tomorrow," Nishiyama said, hovering around me clingingly. He looked distraught.

This was why people liked him so much, I thought. You didn't often find someone as candid and genuine as he was.

"I'm going back to my own life, but I'll never forget you. Thank you for everything. I'll go the day after tomorrow," I said, feeling like crying, too. But the difference between Nishiyama and me was that I didn't let myself.

"Okay. I wish you wouldn't, but I guess you've got to catch the tide. I know it's the right thing for you," he said, and sniffed. "We'll meet again, it's not

like you're dying. I'm going to miss you so much . . ."
He busied himself in prep as though to distract himself, but from time to time he sighed and looked
downcast.

I felt strangely gratified. As brief as it had been,
my presence here had left a definite mark.

And though I doubted I could ever live as freely
as he did, I knew I also wanted to set out toward a
life where I could live more truly as I was.

The next day, I was nodding off to sleep while writing a note to leave for my uncle, when a car horn
sounded on the street outside the window.

The vaguely familiar sound rang out inside my
dream.

In it, I was back under a sweet milky winter sky
with Takanashi. *Hey, it was all just a bad dream.
We're still together. See? You picked me up in the car,
and now we'll go get something to eat, and chat about
nothing, and tell each other we'll be together always.
I knew it was some kind of mistake. You just couldn't
tell me the truth in front of her. Thank God,* I thought
in the dream, and I was smiling, but I could feel my
eyes were full of tears.

The car horn blared again, and I woke up.

I went to the window and looked down, and there was Takanashi's car, as though it had rolled out of the dream.

I won't lie—I was so overjoyed I would have run out into the street without a second glance. *He's here,* I thought, *he came back, he wants me after all. We spent so long building what we had together, I knew it couldn't be over.*

But reality burst my bubble almost instantly. To my disbelief, the face looking out the driver's side window was Nishiyama's. I rushed downstairs with a mix of feelings.

"How did you get this?" I said. "Did you steal it?"

"It's for you. I told him to pay you back your million yen, and he said he'd give you the car. The documents are all in the glove box. His parents can help you sort out the insurance. He said it was the least he could do," Nishiyama said.

"But . . ." I was flummoxed by this extraordinary turn of events. "So you talked to him?"

"Uh-huh. I told him not to worry about you because you were with me now," Nishiyama said. "Sure, I lied. I said he should pay back the money, but he said there was no way he could get it together.

So I said he should give us the car he bought with it, and he agreed pretty quickly. He seems like an okay guy. I thought he'd be really obnoxious."

"Would you say so? I must have seen something in him, I guess," I said, and laughed. "Then again, maybe he only went along with it because he thought you were some kind of thug."

"I don't think that was it. He was still surprised you went to see him, and he said he'd dealt with things badly, and was sorry to have hurt you. He wanted to make amends in some way if there was anything he could do. If you wanted the car then that would be a weight off his mind. So it all worked out."

I started to feel like none of this really mattered anymore; that it all sounded fair enough. It was obvious from Nishiyama's expression that in his mind, this settled everything.

"I'm not sure about this car. It probably smells of her now. Maybe I could sell it," I said.

"You can think it over once you're back home. Do you want to get in? Let's go for a little drive. You haven't even been to the big park here yet, have you?" Nishiyama smiled at me, and so, without thinking too hard about it, I got into the car I'd only ever ridden in with Takanashi.

Immediately, I was beset by more memories: the view from the passenger seat, the feel of the seat belt, the sweep of the window . . . But it was Nishiyama in the seat next to me. Thinner than Takanashi, and not quite as good a driver.

No, this is now, I thought. *Things are okay now.*

I pulled myself together and looked around the car. I noticed how the exterior had been freshly washed, the inside detailed, the ashtray cleared, and the tank filled up, and felt a deep gratitude toward Nishiyama. It meant so much precisely because he didn't know how much it would help me, and had done it anyway. Not because he was trying to please me, but because he was a sensitive person who lived his life this way.

I felt another weight lifted from me, and started mulling over enjoyable things, like how I could drive tomorrow instead of getting the train, and where I would park the car when I got home.

Before my eyes, an unfamiliar city drifted past.

From tomorrow on, I'll only ever be a visitor here. The person I thought I was going to be with will be here with someone else. Life's full of surprises, but this was a big twist, and I'm still reeling, a little, but I'm glad it gave me the chance to spend some time here. I

*got to work in a bar, learn about jazz, and see a differ-
ent way of living—almost like I was an exchange student. All this because I was lucky and met a wonderful
guide,* I reflected, gazing at the city as it flowed by.

"That guy, though. Did he have any idea how
deeply you think about things? What you want in
life, and how you come across kind of happy-go-
lucky, but you're actually a lot more observant and
mature than you seem? I get the impression he
didn't know the half of you, even after all that time,"
Nishiyama said.

"Do you think so? I'm sure we talked about that
kind of thing, you know, over the years."

"Well, from the look on his face, I don't think
he was listening. There's not much to him. He's the
kind of man who only judges a woman by the way
she looks."

"Surely that's going a little too far."

"Trust me, he doesn't respect women and will
always try to control his partners."

"Huh . . . I guess it's a good thing we broke up,
then."

"Seriously, I recognize the type. People like
him only see the world through assumptions. Just
because they know someone who doesn't get to go

outside, or leave their hometown, or has a life that looks boring... To then think that person's mind must be captive, too, or placid and simple? It's such a failure of imagination. But that's how most people think. They don't realize that your mind can be as spacious and as wide-open as you want. Most people don't even try to see the treasure that lies inside the people they know," Nishiyama said.

Of course—he was talking about himself, what he believed.

The car drove through the gate of a big park and cruised down a wide avenue. I hadn't even known there was a space like this in the city. It was a weekday, so the park wasn't crowded, but groups of children chattered on their way home from school, mothers pushed strollers, student couples sat on benches on quiet dates, and runners slipped swiftly past us.

We came to a stop where huge ginkgo trees lined the road on both sides.

It was a breathtaking sight. Fallen leaves formed banks on the ground beneath the trees leading into the distance, and everything was yellow. The whole scene was bathed in sunlight, and drifts of leaves covered the road surface delicately, like a golden snowfall, and disappeared into the distance.

"It's beautiful," I said.

"Doesn't it remind you of snow?" Nishiyama
said.

I got out of the car and strode away from it, my
shoes rustling the dry leaves. I relished their pleasant smell, their weightlessness.

The light washed over the trees. We were practically the only ones there, and the atmosphere felt
holy, as though we really were in a snowy landscape,
or in heaven. The leaves, which came almost to my
knees, were springy underfoot, and flew into the air
on the breath of a whisper. The soft layers absorbed
everything. Far away I heard birdcalls and sounds of
the city. Nishiyama got us hot coffee from a vending
machine, and we traipsed around for a long time,
swishing through the leaves and getting our knees
dirty like children.

There was no past, no future, no words, nothing—
just the light and the yellow and the scent of dry
leaves in the sun.

The entire time, I felt surrounded by happiness.

The next morning, I got in the car and went home.

My family must have agreed to act as though

nothing had happened. My parents greeted me like they always did. My sister was out on a date. Mom and Dad didn't say much about the car except that they'd help me get the paperwork in order.

"I'm going to get out to all kinds of places in this thing," I told them, and laughed. I meant it.

I wasn't sure why, but I didn't feel that upset anymore. And when I went to my room, it felt like a stranger's room.

My sister came home as I was pulling old photographs out of their frames and tearing them up.

She smiled and said, "It's been boring here without you."

I told her that since it seemed like I was going to be here a while anyway, I'd take her out for a drive and something good to eat soon, to make up for leaving her to take care of things while I was gone. Her face lit up in childish delight.

I couldn't help but feel that things had turned out for the best. I knew it was all thanks to Nishiyama and the things he had said.

Missing Nishiyama, I gave him a call the following night.

"Thank you for everything," I said.

"You're welcome. It was my pleasure," he said.

He must have been in the middle of prep. I heard the clank of the lid of the pressure cooker, which he used daily for cozy dishes like *oden* and braised daikon.

I cast my mind back to the view of cars on the main street from the window of my room above Cul-de-Sac, the last window on the dead-end road. At dusk the shops in the alley would switch on their lights and come floating up out of the gloom. When I went downstairs Nishiyama would be preparing to open. The whole place would smell enticingly of the appetizer he was serving that day, and the counter would be neat and orderly. In my mind's eye I could see it all.

"Tell me your address once you get settled in Tokyo. I'll come visit if I'm ever in town."

"I will."

Even as we said those words, we both knew that now that those carefree days were behind us, we were unlikely to see each other again.

That time had been a gift from fortune, like a blanket gently laid over me by the heavens.

It had been suffused with a rare joy, like if you'd

made a curry, and thrown in some leftover yogurt and spices, apples, maybe some extra onion on a whim, and ended up—on a one-in-a-million chance—with a dish that was immeasurably delicious, but which you had no chance of re-creating.

It had been an interlude that had shone so brightly only because I hadn't expected anything from anyone and hadn't needed to accomplish anything.

Realizing this only deepened my sadness and gratitude.

"I just wanted to thank you for everything. I don't know how, but I had a really great time there. I'll remember it for the rest of my life," I said.

"No, I enjoyed it too. Thanks for giving me my best memories of this place," Nishiyama said, and there was a wobble in his voice. He was more sentimental than people realized.

But I knew that before long, he'd forget about the time we'd shared, and deftly start making his way through his next life.

"Thanks for the car. I've decided to keep it."

"I definitely think that's the right call. It'll make things easier for him as well."

"Take care of yourself."

"You too. Have a good life!"

"Keep looking out for happiness. Don't stop," I said, and my tears were coming, too. I hung up and cried for just a minute. These were good tears: an offering to accidents of timing. They squeezed my chest and glittered, and out of my sadness they fell and fell.

I knew that under our separate skies, Nishiyama and I were both so lonely it physically hurt. And in my mind's eye I saw once again the view from the upstairs window, and the quiet golden world where ginkgo leaves fell and settled forever on the ground.

I felt then that—even if I might someday forget when and where I had encountered them, or how they'd made me feel—these scenes were safely stowed in the part of my heart where I kept my most treasured memories, and would be among the visions that rose, radiant, to meet me at the moment of my death, as symbols of happiness, to lead me away.

BANANA YOSHIMOTO is the author of the international bestseller *Kitchen*. She has published eleven books in English translation, including *Moshi Moshi* and *Dead-End Memories*. She was born in Tokyo in 1964 and graduated from Nihon University College of Art, where she majored in literature. She debuted as a writer in 1987 with *Kitchen*, a novella that won her the Kaien Newcomer Writers Prize. In 1988, *Moonlight Shadow*, her thesis story, was awarded the Izumi Kyoka Prize for Literature. Then in 1989, she received two accolades: the Minister of Education's Art Encouragement Prize for New Artists for *Kitchen* and *Utakata/Sanctuary* and the Yamamoto Shugoro Prize for *Goodbye Tsugumi*. In 1995, she won the Murasaki Shikibu Prize for *Amrita*, a full-length novel. And in 2000, *Furin to Nambei*, a collection of stories set in South America, received the Bunkamura Deux Magots Literary Prize. Most recently, in 2022, she won the Tanizaki Prize for *Miton to Fubin*. Her work has been translated and published in more than thirty countries, and she has won several awards outside of Japan. In Italy, she won the Scanno Literary Prize in 1993, the Fendissime Literary Prize in 1996, the Maschera d'Argento Prize in 1999, and the Capri Award in 2011. You can follow her on Instagram at @bananayoshimoto2017.

ASA YONEDA is the translator of Banana Yoshimoto's *Dead-End Memories* and *Moshi Moshi*, as well as *Idol, Burning* by Rin Usami and *The Lonesome Bodybuilder* by Yukiko Motoya.